# The Panther on Cold Mountain
*and Other Stories*

*Charles C. Fletcher*

Published By
**FLETCHER BOOKS**
2310 Harris Circle NW
Cleveland, TN 37311

© 2009 by Charles C. Fletcher.

All rights reserved. No part of this book may be reproduced, stored in a retrieval system or transmited in any form or by any means without the prior written permission of the publishers, except by a reviewer who may quote brief passages in a review to be printed in newspaper, magazine or journal.

Second Printing

All characters in this book are fictitious, and any resemblance to real persons, living or dead, is coincidental.

ISBN: 978-1-933251-75-2
Published by Fletcher Books
Cleveland, Tennessee, USA

Printed in the United States of America

# Foreword

As you read the stories in this book, take into account that the writer does not consider himself an author or a writer. He does think that he is a "storyteller" as were most all of the people who lived in the mountains of Western North Carolina before, during, and after the Great Depression of the 1930s. The younger generation who came along after WW II were not exposed to these storytellers and have no idea of what life was like during what we old-timers like to call "the good old days".

With this in mind, I decided to continue telling about the things that I remember and were told to me when I was growing up. These events start where the others ended in the my first book titled *Out West and Back*.

These stories are based on actual events as I remember them. Because of my age (eighty-six), I sometimes have to tax my mind to remember what happened and where. I sometimes have to consult with my eighty-five year-old younger brother, 'TJ' (also known as 'TP') for dates, places, and names.

I tell these stories to make the younger generation of today aware of the hardships we older people faced in getting to this point in our lives. What you read in these stories is a part of what aunts, uncles, grandpas, grandmas, and all the others not having all the modern things we have today experienced. If I did not record these events of my life, they would be lost forever. My hope is that, in reading my stories, young people will learn about the past and that older people will refresh their memories of, "the good old days".

# Table of Contents

The Panther On Cold Mountain ..................................................... 11
The Gambler And The Chicken ..................................................... 17
Trading Cows ................................................................................ 22
The Chestnut Tree ......................................................................... 27
Black Water .................................................................................. 31
Burma Doctor ............................................................................... 35
Mountain Medicine ....................................................................... 43
Medicine Show, 1930s ................................................................. 47
Gone Hunting, 1936 ..................................................................... 51
Fishing Trip .................................................................................. 56
Prayer Meeting ............................................................................. 64
Full-time Preacher ........................................................................ 67
The Radio ..................................................................................... 74
Train Rides ................................................................................... 77
Hog Killing Time ......................................................................... 83
Saturday Night Bath .................................................................... 87
Wash Day, 1930s ......................................................................... 90
Haints, Ghosts, And Boogers ...................................................... 94
Friends ........................................................................................ 100
Labor Day, 1930s ....................................................................... 104
Saturday, 1930s .......................................................................... 109
Huckleberry Picking .................................................................. 114
Ramp Tramp ............................................................................... 120
Biscuits And Gravy .................................................................... 124
A Wife For Life .......................................................................... 129
Odd Names And Places ............................................................. 133
Election Time, 1930s ................................................................. 139
Possum Dinner ........................................................................... 143
Skunk Doctor ............................................................................. 149
Afterword ................................................................................... 159
Biographical Note ...................................................................... 160

# The Panther on Cold Mountain
## and Other Stories

# The Panther On Cold Mountain

The following story was told to my sisters, my brother, and me on more occasions than I can remember. For entertainment in the winter months, all of our family would gather around the big rock fireplaces to keep warm and pop corn over a blazing fire of big logs. We enjoyed this, but the best part of the evening before retiring for the night was the stories that Dad or Mom would tell. They would start by saying, "Now what I'm about to tell you is true. I know it is, because...."

It didn't make any difference to us if we had heard a story before. Every time the stories were told they changed a little bit, and they were always exciting. Once the story started, we children moved in as close as we could get. On this particular night it was Dad's turn to tell the story—

"It was in 1919 or 1920 when my family were living in the settlement called Crusoe. Crusoe is on the East Fork of the Pigeon River at the foot of Cold Mountain. At that time, all of my kinfolk lived on or around this mountain. The land belonged to them."

"I have a cousin, Wes Pless, who spent a lot of his time on Cold Mountain hunting black bear. He was known as the best bear hunter in these mountains. Cold Mountain and all the other mountains were then owned by the people who lived on them. They were later sold, and the Pisgah National Park took ownership of them. This stopped a lot of the bear hunting trips because the land was closed to hunters. Wes had been on a bear hunt one fall, and when he returned home he told me this story:"

"'I know you won't believe this, but I saw one of the biggest black panthers that I ever saw. I've seen mountain lions, wild cats, coons, fox, bear, and a lot of small animals on this mountain, but that was the biggest panther I have ever seen. In fact, that is the first black panther I've ever seen. Boy was he pretty, slick, and black. He really shined when daylight hit him.'"

"'You know something,' he said. 'Black Panthers don't live here in this country; they come from across the ocean. From some place like Africa or Asia. Glad we don't have them running around everywhere in this country. They have panthers in Florida, but they ain't as big and mean as them African black panthers.'"

"'When I was in Waynesville about a month ago to pay my taxes, I heard some fellers talking about a panther. One said that it run away from a circus that was in Asheville a while back. He said that it was a she and it was going to have some little ones soon. He said she ain't dangerous unless you bother her. The man that run the circus said he would give anyone fifty dollars if he would ketch her. I wouldn't even get close to that thing for fifty dollars.'"

"You know what?" Dad said. "Wes had me all worked up about that panther. I'd never seen one, but I was determined to get a look at the one on Cold Mountain. Yes, sir. I was gonna look for that big cat."

"This was before your mom and me were married. I had hunted all over them mountains all by myself. If that panther was still around, I would find him."

"The next morning I went over to where Wes lived. 'Wes' I said, 'can I take loan of one of your bear guns? I'm going looking for that panther. Thought I should take a more powerful gun than my old 22. Might have to shoot that thing.'"

"'You can take one of my 30-30s. They're powerful. And you'd better take another hand-full of shells. Can't never tell what you might run into.'"

"I was on my way. I took the sled road up to where the last family lived on Cold Mountain. From there on up the mountain I had to pick every which way I could find. The going was tough, but I was all set to see that animal that Wes said he saw on Cold Mountain."

"I had walked for several hours, and by looking at where the sun was I knew that it was way after dinner time, and I was beginning to get a little hungry. So I found a good place to set down under a big chestnut tree. That tree must have been a hundred feet tall and as big around as a wagon wheel."

"I took out one of my biscuits with ham in it and began eating. I had packed two of them in a poke that morning. They were left over from our breakfast. They shore tasted good. All that walking and climbing up that mountain sure makes a man hungry."

"I was soon through eating and on my way again. 'Not much farther to the top,' I said. 'And it's getting late in the day. I'd better start looking for a good place to sleep.'"

"I didn't dare go down this mountain after dark. I didn't bring a lantern, and if you can't see where you are going, its dangerous. There are rock cliffs that go straight down for fifty feet, and a body could walk off one of them real easy in the dark."

"'I'll get a good night's sleep and look around some more tomorrow. I've slept out on these mountains a many a time. Nothing going to bother a person. Besides I've got this gun and a pocket full of bullets.'"

"I found a level place against a big chestnut tree that was lying on the ground. Must have blown down. I cut some branches from a fir tree to make a bed against that tree. I was getting hungry again, but I only had one biscuit and ham left. 'Better save this for breakfast,' I said."

"The sun had gone down over the top of the mountain, and it was getting pretty dark. 'Better get settled to bed,' I said. 'Morning will be here before you know it.'"

"I didn't need any cover. It had been a bright, sunny day, and the ground was good and warm. I was asleep in nothing flat."

"It was way past midnight when I woke up. 'Something is different.' I thought. 'I don't remember covering myself these leaves and sticks. Something strange is going on here. This never has happened before, and I've slept out in the woods a many a time.'"

Dad stood up. Took his pipe from his shirt pocket, dumped the ashes, on the hearth, and began to fill the pipe with fresh tobacco.

"Better get to bed," he said. "Not long 'til morning. You boys have to get up early. TJ has to milk the cow, and Charles has got to feed the hogs and build a fire in the cook stove. You girls have to get up, too. Tomorrow is another school day." He then took some straws from a can to light his pipe with.

"Don't stop now," I said. "Finish the story before we go to bed."

The other children also were asking him to finish.

"I'll finish tomorrow after we finish eating supper and get the evening work done. Go on now. Get to bed."

We knew that he would not finish his story that night. He had done this on several occasions before. He kept us guessing about what would happen next. TJ and I climbed the ladder to the attic of the log house we lived in. This was where he and I slept. We were in bed really quick. It was very cold up there because there were chinks between the logs, and the cold wind was going through the loft.

The following day was the usual: up early, build the fires, milk the cow, do the feeding, and then off to school. Only this day seemed to go by a little slower than the other days. I guess we were anxious to get home and hear what covered dad with leaves and sticks.

When we had finished our chores for the day, eaten supper, and taken our places by the fire, TJ and I were ready for the rest of the story.

"I'll wait until Mom and the girls get the dishes put away and the kitchen cleaned. Then I'll finish the story."

"You women hurry up in there," I yelled... "If you don't get in here soon it'll be bed time, and we'll never find out what put the leaves on Dad. Come on now, and bring the corn popper. We may get a little hungry."

Here they came. They took their regular places around the fire, and everybody was really quiet.

"We're ready for the story," I said. "Hope you don't leave anything out."

"Well," he began, "like I said, I'd never had anything like this happen to me before. No sir. I was aiming to figure this out."

"I found a piece of a log about the size of me, and. I picked it up and laid it exactly where I'd been sleeping. I put the leaves over it, then the sticks. It looked just like me laying there." Then I picked up the gun, moved up the side of the mountain about fifty feet, and sat down close to a big tree. I got the biscuit with the ham out of my pocket and began eating my breakfast. I was hungry again already."

"I had just finished eating when I heard a noise down below where I had been sleeping. It was getting daylight, and I could see pretty well. I let the safety off on the gun. I kind of squinted my eyes and took a good look toward the noise. There it was, plain as daylight. It was that black cat that Wes was telling about. You know what? There were two of the curtest little black kittens that you ever saw along with her. She had started her a family."

"The kittens stopped. The momma panther got down low on the ground and crept toward where I had slept last night. All of a sudden she leaped about twenty feet in the air and landed on that log that I had covered up to look like me. She tore that log into a million pieces in nothing flat. I'm glad that it was the log instead of me."

"The two kittens come running to where the momma was expecting to get something to eat for their breakfast. They were as disappointed as their mom: nothing there but splinters from the log."

"I now had it all figured out. The black panther had covered me and gone to get her kittens. They were planning on eating me."

"I could have killed that panther, but I thought for a few minutes. 'If I kill her, the two kittens will starve to death. And besides, any animal that was that pretty didn't need to be killed.'"

"I made a noise with my feet in the leaves. That panther turned and looked straight at me. Her eyes looked like balls of fire, real shinny. Well, my look was short. The whole family disappeared in the laurel thicket in about one second."

"Wes had said the fellers he heard talking this creature in Waynesville were saying that a full grown panther could jump twenty-five feet backwards and straight up and close to fifty forward."

"Well, I had found what I was looking for and was ready to head for home. I went up Cold Mountain many times after that trip to find a panther. I saw and killed lots of animals, but I'll never forget that panther that I saw on Cold Mountain."

Dad told this story several times the fireplace when I was growing up in the mountains of Western North Carolina. Every time that he told the story, it was a little different, but he always declared, "I'll swear that this really happened to me."

# The Gambler And The Chicken

Since the time of Adam and Eve, it seems that the nature of man is to want something for nothing. There are many ways trying to get something for nothing, but the one that is most popular is gambling. That is to say, "I'll beat the odds." Or, "I know I can win." It has always been this way, and will continue to be in the future. Columbus was told that the world was flat and if he sailed far enough to the east that his ships would drop off the edge of the world. Old Columbus said, "I'll take a chance".

Recently while visiting my brother TJ in North Carolina we were discussing how the price of mountain land had increased over the past fifty years.

"You know," he said. "I could have bought the old Aunt Hass Clark home and the mountain for $6,000 a few years back. Do you know that those people from Florida are now paying thousand of dollars for a small spot to build a summer home."

"Why didn't you buy it from Aunt Hass?" I said. "As I remember you were always a gambler. Even when we were in grade school you tried to win everyone's marbles."

"That all changed several years ago. Let me tell you a story about my gambling. As you said, I always thought that I could beat anyone at his 'game of chance", and I always thought it was easier to do that than having to work for something."

He then began his story:

"When I went into military service during World War II, I came into contact with real gamblers. Professionals. The ones who could convince you that you would win against all odds.

With some spare time between my duties I thought, "Why not? I will win lots of money and send it home. When this war is over I'll have me some money when I get home. This was my first experience with 'big time' gambling."

"The war soon ended, and I returned home to Canton, my little hometown in the mountains of Western North Carolina. One of the first things to be done was to get a wife. I didn't have to look around too much because I had made my mind up as to who I wanted for a wife. I went to school with the girl I had in mind, and she also lived in the same community that I lived in. Her name was Alveta Medford. She would be the one, if she would marry me. "

"The time came for me to muster up enough courage to ask her. 'What if she says no? Never know what she will say. Better get it over with.'"

"She said 'yes', and we began planning. Time was short, and the big day soon came. We were 'man and wife'. I forgot all about the gambling thing until I began working in the paper mill that was in Canton. It seems that gambling shows up in places you would never think it would."

"Being newly married, I needed to earn and save all the money that I could. We wanted to build a new home on some land I had bought. Alveta and I saved as well as we could, but there was the buying of food and clothing."

"Alveta said, "Why don't we get a few chickens? We wouldn't have to buy eggs, and maybe we'd have enough to sell.'"

"'Good idea,' I said."

"I began to shop around for a few hens and a rooster. One of our neighbors had more chickens than he needed, so he offered to sell me a few."

"'How much for the hens,' I said."

"'Well, seeing that you are just getting started as a newly wedded man, I'll let you have twelve hens for six dollars, and I'll throw in a rooster for free.'"

"'It's a deal,' I said."

"He caught the hens and put them in a wooden box. This was the easy part. He then went after the rooster, but that big red bird wasn't going to go nowhere. He ruffled his feathers and made a dive toward his master. When he was close, the boss made a quick grab and had him by the legs. Into the box with the hens he went. I gave him the six dollars and headed home.

We were now the proud owners of a chicken farm, and we were on our way to getting rich selling eggs. They would bring fifteen to twenty cents a dozen."

"All went well for a while except that rooster had it in for me. Every time I went to gather the eggs, he would try flogging me. I would give him a kick, and he would back off."

"We soon experienced a shortage in eggs in the nests. We didn't know where they were going until one day Alveta saw a dog coming out of the hen house with an egg in his mouth. It seemed that he knew exactly when each hen had laid an egg. We threw rocks to run him away, but he would slip back when we were not watching. I was buying eggs at the store for thirty cents a dozen and chicken feed at a dollar a bag. This was a loosing deal."

"'Got to think of something to get my six dollars that I paid for those chickens back.'"

"There was a fellow at the paper mill where I worked who had a gambling thing going. He would have 'tip boards' that he sold chances from for money and anything else he wanted to make a profit on."

"'That's the answer,' I said. 'I'll run them chickens off on a tip board.'"

"One evening after I finished my shift at the mill, I headed to Smokey Mountain Wholesale to purchase tip boards. I was about to get back in the gambling business."

"The boards were a quarter each. There were fifty chances on each board. At ten cents a chance, that would earn five dollars. This would get me four dollars and seventy-five cents for each chicken. 'What a good profit,' I thought."

"The first chicken to be sold on the tip board was a big black hen. She was fat and would make a big pan of southern fried chicken or a big pot of chicken and dumplings. What a deal. I would tell all the prospective gamblers."

"All went well until I tried to catch that old black hen. She must have known something fishy was going on, and she didn't want any part of it. I sold forty of the fifty tickets, and the ones that had bought wanted me to open the seal to she who the winner was before going home."

"'OK,' I said. 'What if the winning number is still on the board?'"

"'Then you win your hen.'"

"Off came the seal, and (you guessed it) I was the winner of my old black hen."

"Alveta gave me a hard time about the gambling, so I agreed to take the chickens to the Farmer's Federation. This was a farm supply store that bought and sold chickens. They would pay me fifty cents each for the chickens." After they went in the chicken house to roost on a Friday night, I caught them, tied their legs together, and put them in a big box. On Saturday morning I was on my way to the store to sell the chickens that we were going to get rich off of from selling eggs."

"Again, that old black hen gave me a rough time. She somehow got her legs untied, and when I opened the box out she jumped and out the door of the store she ran. I gave the others to the clerk and said that I would catch the one that got loose. I went outside and saw that black hen sitting under the store. Under I went, crawling on my knees, bumping my head, and never noticing that the store had piled their coal for their heater under the store. The farther I crawled, the farther that chicken went. I happened to notice that I was black with coal dust and spider webs."

"'What am I doing?' I said. 'I've ruined a good pair of pants that cost a dollar and my best shirt that cost fifty cents. What for?' I thought. 'All this for a fifty-cent hen.' I crawled out from under the store, went inside, got my six dollars, and headed home."

"As soon as Alveta saw me, the world began to come apart. 'Where have you been? What happened to you?' These were only a few of her remarks before I had a chance to explain."

"I told her what happened, and then she began again. 'It serves you right, your trying to gamble them chickens away, when you know good and well that gambling is a sin. I hope you have learned a lesson. Just look at you. Them good clothes will never wash clean again.'"

"Soon everything was quiet. I had learned my lesson That old black hen had taught me that gambling and chickens don't go together."

# Trading Cows

I guess it is also the nature of man to barter and trade with someone with the intention of getting the better of the deal. This was true of my dad. He would trade anything he had always thinking that he was getting the better part of the deal.

There was one such deal that he did when I was about ten years old that I will never forget. It was a deal that involved our only source of milk and butter. This was our big jersey cow that gave our family nearly ten quarts of rich milk twice every day. Once each morning and again that evening my brother TJ did the milking, and there was so much milk that he couldn't carry it to the house. TJ was only nine years old. Mom had to go to the barn and bring the milk to the house.

We never had the faintest idea that this member of our family would be involved in one of Dad's "swapping deals." But our cow was about to move to a new home. It happened at a time when Mom was visiting her mom and dad. She was gone for only one day, but the setting was perfect for one of the biggest and worst trades that Dad ever made.

A drinking buddy of Dad's came to visit the day that Mom was away visiting. His name was Jack Blankenship. He lived in the old Sam Robinson home place off the Thickety Road. It was a short ways from the Oak Grove Baptist Church. We were living in an area known as "Hainty Hollow." Lots of people stayed away from this area at night. They were superstitious and believed all the scary things that they had heard about ghosts that were in the near by graveyard. We lived there for several years and never saw any ghosts, but we children would not go near the graveyard after dark.

Well Jack and Dad were standing at a big spring that was at the foot of a big maple tree. We had a spring box there where Mom kept her milk and butter in the cool water that was flowing from the spring. The refrigerator was not a common thing in the home at this time (the 1930s) where we lived. The spring box was also where Dad usually kept a half gallon fruit jar of homemade moonshine, (corn liquor). It was where he entertained his friends when they came to visit. I think this was the reason that he had a good bit of visitors. They enjoyed the cool spring water that they used to get the sting from their throat caused by the "white lightning." Here was the perfect time and place for Jack to get him a good cow and get rid of the one he had that was going dry.

Now our cow had come to the drain from the spring for a drink of water.

"Say, Fletch? How would you trade that cow of yours for a real good cow that will have a calf pretty soon? You could probably get four or five dollars for the calf if it's a heifer. If it's a bull calf you can feed it real good for about six months and kill it for veal. Probably get a hundred cans from it."

He wasn't as far along with the drinking as Dad was, so he was taking advantage of this to make a trade.

"Well, my cow won't have a calf for quite some time, and I could use an extra five dollars. I'll trade with you. I'll get one of the boys to go home with you and bring your cow back."

The deal was made and, I went with Jack and brought back the new cow. Mom came home a little before dark, and one of the first things she saw was the strange animal.

"That's our cow," TJ said. "Dad and Jack Blankenship traded cows today. Don't know why though. Our old cow gave plenty of milk and it was pretty rich. Had about two inches of cream on a bucketful. Dad just likes to do some trading, I guess."

She told Dad, "You take that cow back this very minute and bring my cow home."

"I can't go tonight. I'll talk to Jack tomorrow."

"You'd better", Mom said. "TJ, you'd better go and milk her if we have to wait until tomorrow to take her back to Jack."

TJ got a big two and a half gallon bucket and headed to the barn. He wasn't gone long until he came back to the house with the milk. He didn't have to have Mom come carry the milk to the house because he had milked only about one gallon from this cow. It was nothing like the big bucket of milk from our cow that Dad had traded.

Mom began to cry. "We won't have enough milk, and I can't give the Holland family any. Their little children will be without milk because they don't own a cow. And this milk is so skimpy that I won't have any cream to churn to make butter for the table. How could anyone be stupid enough to trade a good cow for one that is skin and bones and doesn't give enough milk for our family?"

Dad hung his head down, and out the door he went. I followed him and said, "You'd better think of some way to get our cow back, or you'll never see any peace of mind around here."

"I know," he said. "The first thing tomorrow morning you make a trip to Jack's house. When no one is around, you tell him that I have some mighty fine peach brandy, and if he would come over, I'll let him sample it. This will get him to come, and I'll think of someway to get our cow back."

Sure enough, Jack was at our house around dinner time. His twelve year old son, Willard, came, too, so he could visit with TJ and me. Mom invited them to eat with us, but they said they were not hungry. Dad rushed through his meal and headed to the spring box and to the moonshine that he had added peach flavoring to. Jack was right behind him, and it was not long until they were sampling the "peach brandy."

After about an hour and a dozen samples of the brandy, Dad and Jack were doing a lot of talking. Dad had made it a point to not drink very much but gave Jack all he wanted.

"Say, Jack," Dad began. How would you trade me my cow back? The old woman is having a fit over me letting you have her."

"I don't know," Jack said with a slur in his speech. "My old woman likes that cow. Haven't had this much milk from any cow that I've owned before."

Dad saw right away that Jack wasn't about to part with his new cow without some kind of a bargain.

"Tell you what I'll do," Dad said. "I'll give you your cow back and throw in one of them OIC pigs out in the hog lot."

"I don't know," Jack said. "I guess I could use a hog for our winter meat. We don't have one. I don't want to part with this good cow, but seeing as to the trouble you are in with your old woman, I'll trade with you."

"Go get a sack," Dad told TJ. Need something to carry the pig over to Jack's house. Put a halter on the cow. You and Charles can go with Jack and Willard and bring our cow back."

Off we went, Willard with the pig in the sack thrown over his shoulder and TJ leading the cow. Jack was staggering along behind. That peach brandy was working on old Jack.

It was during the summer months, and it was pretty warm. We had traveled to "Home Brew Knob," about half way, , when Jack said, "I need to stop and rest."

Willard took the sack with the pig in it off his shoulder and laid it on the ground. "This pig has finally quit kicking. Must've gone to sleep."

Willard opened the sack to take a peek. "Dad, I believe the pig is dead," said Willard.

"No, son. He's not dead; he's resting. Close that sack and let's get on home."

When we reached Jack's house, Willard set the sack with the pig in it on the ground. "Dad, I believe this pig is really dead."

"If he's dead, you're the one who killed him. Take him to the pig pen and let him go. He'll be OK."

Willard emptied the sack, but the pig didn't move. He hollered to his Dad, "This pig is dead! What do you want me to do with him?"

"Willard, you killed my pig," he said to his son. "We can't waste that good meat. Bring him to the house. I'll dress him, and we will eat him for supper."

TJ and I put the halter on our old cow and started to make our way back home. TJ said, "I bet Dad won't ever trade off our cow again."

Anyhow, everyone was happy. Mom had her cow back, and Jack and his family made the best supper that they'd had in a long time out of that dead pig.

# The Chestnut Tree

The old timers used to tell of the times when the chestnut trees would bloom in the spring and their white flowers would make the sides of the mountains look like it had snowed.

Not only did the wildlife of the forest, such as bears, deer, squirrels, and birds, depend on the nuts from these giant nut-bearing trees, the people of these mountains did, too. They would use them to feed their farm animals and for many other things in the home. They would fatten their beef and pork for their winter meats with chestnuts. Chestnuts were dried and made into meal for baking bread. They were boiled, roasted, and dried for eating. Some were eaten raw. Not only were the chestnuts tasty with their sweet flavor, but they were high in nutrition.

The chestnut tree was often used as lumber. It had a straight grained wood that was as rot resistant as the redwood tree. These mighty trees were used in railroad cross ties, furniture, houses, barns and for many other uses. The tree would reach about 100 feet in height and would have a diameter of about five or six feet. It would be fifty feet from the ground up to the first branch on the tree.

Many tales were told about these big trees. There were records of some having a diameter of eight feet. Just one tree, sawed into lumber, would make a full load for a train rail car. It was the "king" tree of the forest, not only in the mountains where I grew up, but also in many other states of the southeast. These trees were so plentiful that everyone thought that they would be here forever.

In the early part of the 20th Century, around the year of 1904, we noticed that something was wrong with these large trees. They were all starting to die. It was discovered that the trees had a strange fungus they didn't have a resistance to. It was a fungus that had entered the US from Asia. It moved from New York State to the southern states at a rapid rate. The fungus helped destroy the old chestnut trees.

Also, the lumber industry was going full blast, cutting these giant trees for their lumber. They would only take the better part of the tree from the ground up to the first branches. The rest would be left in the forest to rot. Pulp mills were using the chestnut for its tannic acid, for leather tanning, and making paper from the pulp after the acid was removed. One of the larger mills was in the area was the Champion Fiber Company, located in our town of Canton, North Carolina. Canton was my home for many years.

Champion owned most of what is now the Pisgah National Forest as well as the area from the Cherokee Indian Reservation to the Tennessee state line at the top of the mountains now a part of one of the most visited parks in the United States, The Great Smokey Mountains National Park. They cut the trees under the name of Sunburst Logging Company. Sunburst Logging was owned by Peter G. Thomson who lived in Ohio.

There was also a lumber company in Tennessee that was cutting the trees from their side of the mountains in the area that would later be the Great Smokey Mountain National Park. This company was called the Little River Lumber Company. It was owned by Colonel Townsend. With these two big companies logging in the mountains, the chestnut trees were disappearing at a very fast pace. The cutting didn't cease until President Franklin D. Roosevelt made the area a national park and stopped the cutting of trees.

I will never forget the first trip that I made to the mountains to gather chestnuts. It was on a Sunday when Dad said, "After dinner, we'll go up Crusoe to Cold Creek where Wes lives and gather some chestnuts."

Wes was the husband of a cousin of mine. He and his brothers, sisters, and the rest of the Pless family owned most of what was known as Cold Mountain. This is one of the mountains that make up the Pisgah Forest today.

After we finished eating our dinner ("lunch" to city folks), Mom found a couple of flower sacks and a couple of pillow cases to take along for gathering the chestnuts. We loaded up in the old "T-Model" Ford and were on our way up winding roads, along the bank of the East Fork of the Pigeon River, up Cold Creek, and to the log house that Wes and his family lived in. After hugs and greetings, Dad told them what one of the reasons for our visit was, picking up chestnuts. Wes pointed to a grove of trees nearby and said, "I think you can find all the chestnuts you want over there. I was out there the other day and the ground was covered with them shinny nuts. Yes-sir, there are a plenty of them."

We children usually went barefooted until it began to frost, but there was no way that you would dare go anywhere near a chestnut tree without shoes on your feet. The burrs that the nuts were buried in had sharp stickers on them, and when one got stuck in your hand or foot it was painful and very hard to remove. So, shoes were a must.

Wes was right about all the many nuts that were under the trees in this chestnut tree grove. It didn't take very long to fill the sacks we had and head back to the house where the grown folks were having a great visit and exchanging the news and happenings that occurred since our last visit. Then, after some more hugs and good-byes, we were on our way back home.

We thought that there were enough nuts to last all winter, but they were all gone by Christmas time. We had eaten them all. We ate them boiled, roasted, raw and even in some bread that Mom made. She also used some in other things she cooked. When roasting them over the fire in the fireplace you had to make a hole in every nut. If you didn't, there would be a big bang. When they got hot, if there was not an escape for the steam inside the nuts, they would blow up and fly all over room. If one hit you it would cause a burn on your skin.

The nuts did have a bad feature. If you ate them without cooking them first, they would cause a lot of gas in your stomach. This was not good, especially if you were going to school. The schoolhouses didn't have cooling or fans. During the chestnut season, the teacher would open all the windows and doors to the room regardless of the weather outside. This was not only for her comfort but for all the students as well. Thank goodness, this only lasted for a week or two.

I made many more trips to the chestnut trees while growing up, and it became very noticeable that something was wrong with the trees. They began to lose their leaves early, and they had many dead limbs. Also, there were not as many nuts as usual.

By the year 1950, all that remained of these beautiful trees was a forest of skeletons that were bare of leaves. The Asian fungus had done its job. All the trees were gone. There is a movement underway today to try to restore the trees to the forests of the southeastern United States. I hope that it is a successful project and that my grandchildren can someday experience and enjoy the chestnut trees as I did as a child. I think that mankind has learned from the mistakes they have made in the past when they butchered our beautiful forest for the sake of wealth. It must never happen again.

# Black Water

I remember the miracle river that ran through our section of Haywood County in the mountains of Western North Carolina. This river, the Pigeon River, satisfied many needs of young people and sometimes older people, too. It was not the normal river you find elsewhere; it was only normal until it entered the paper mill. The natural water was crystal clear with many types of fish and other water wildlife in and around it. All of its water was from the many springs and creeks flowing from what is now the Pisgah National Forest.

There was a dam across the river that diverted it through the mill. After that it wasn't natural anymore. All of the spent chemicals that were used for cooking the wood chips to make pulp for the paper machines was dumped in this beautiful river above the paper mill.

We young boys had a favorite spot on the river that we loved to visit. This was at the mouth of Murray Branch. Murray Branch was a small creek that flowed from Little Sam Mountain into the river. It was a clear, cold stream. Where it entered the river, it had deposited sand made from the many rocks that it had flowed over as it made its way from the mountains. This formed sort of a sandy beach and was the perfect place for a swimming hole.

The water was not too deep at this place on the river. It was only about five feet deep at the most. Because of the paper mill, our "black water" swimming hole was always warm, even on the coldest days of the winter months. We had a year-round swimming hole.

We had to build a fire on the beach on the cold days so we could dry off before putting our clothes back on. This was not a big problem because we only wore denim pants or overalls with a shirt. We never wore any underclothes because we never had any. We always washed off the many chemicals that were on our body from swimming in this black water in Murray Branch. If we didn't wash really well we would have a very bad odor our bodies.

There were other spots for the boys in our community to have fun on this "black river". One was some rocks in a shallow part of the river that were very slick from the chemical deposits on them. It was as if they were coated with some kind of soap. We would slide down these rocks. It was pretty rough on our bottoms.

The river did have some good uses besides swimming and sliding. It had a "healing power." Not only did the boys use it, but sometimes the girls and adults had an occasion to visit our Black Water River, too. It would cure many skin problems: poison ivy rash, itchiness, head lice, and most any other problem with the skin. Also, if our dogs got infected with mange (a skin fungus that animals sometimes had), we took them to that miracle Black Water River, gave them a good dipping, and in no time they were well.

We didn't know about the bad effects of all the chemicals that were in the water. There were chlorine, caustic soda, tannic acid, and many other chemicals in the river that we were not aware of. Nor did we know about all the harm they could be to our health. We only knew that the black water would cure any type of skin and parasite problems we had on our bodies.

Many years later after thinking about the healing power of the black water, I came to the conclusion that it got its healing power from the tannic acid in the water. This was waste from cooking the native chestnut trees for the pulp and the tannic acid that were extracted their wood. Tannic acid was dried to a powder form and sold to the many tanneries that were around in this part of the 20th century (1930s). There was a big demand for tannic acid to use for making leather from the hides of animals.

When we were living in the Crossroad Hill section of the Thickety Community, my grandparents lived in the Phillipsville Community. The Black River separated the two communities. There were two ways for us to get to Grandpa's house. One was to walk to the city limits of Canton and cross a bridge, which was about a three mile trip. The other was to go to the shallows of the river, roll up our britches legs, and wade across. This route was only about one-half mile. This shallow portion of the river was where farmers would cross with their horse drawn wagons or on horseback. Distance didn't mean a whole lot to us then, but we could spend more time visiting and less time walking if we waded across the river, so we took the shorter route.

We all were soon older and were either too busy to go to the river, or we moved away. The nature of the water also changed. It was still black, but its healing power disappeared. All the chestnut trees were gone, so the tannic acid disappeared The southern pine tree had taken over as the main source of pulp for making paper. Waste from the cooked pine wood was in the form of turpentine. It didn't have the medicinal properties that the tannic acid had. And again, new homes were being built that had bathrooms equipped with a bathtub for bathing. All the excitement of the river was disappearing very fast. Also, as time went by, I do not believe any parent would allow their children to even put a foot in that black water.

Times have changed since I was a small boy and also the river has changed again. When I visit today I cross the river and notice that it is not black anymore. The paper mill is still operating, but its waste is removed and treated before the water is put back in the river. I am told that there are fish and other life in the river now. The smell (stench) is not as bad as it was when I worked there after WW II. The smell of the river always offended people who lived in other parts of the world and came there, but to the people who lived there, it was hardly ever noticed or mentioned. After all, the paper mill was the main place where people got their money to buy the things that they needed for living.

We had many "home remedies" for doctoring our aches and pains in those days, but the black water of the river was one of the unusual cures for us in that day and time. I guess we should have bottled up some of it, and we wouldn't have to go to the drugstores today and pay the high prices that they charge.

I could keep writing to no end about our Black Water River, but you would have to have lived as I did and to have experienced the joys of swimming and bathing in this river. I am getting old, and unless I tell you about this river now, you would never know that it existed.

# Burma Doctor

A few years ago I was sent on assignment to Kawerau, New Zealand, to help organize a start-up for a new paper mill that the company I worked for had built there. While I was there, I had many new experiences in my life, but there was one that I will never forget. This was my getting acquainted with the local doctor who was formerly from England, India, and Burma.

After the mill was on line and my help was not required on a twenty-four hour schedule, a couple of the workers asked me to go deer hunting with them. I said I would, so they borrowed a land rover truck from the company, took the battery from my car, got a spot light and a deer gun, and off we went. Their deer hunting was done at night. One person would drive, one would use the spot light, and the another would do the shooting.

We were in the "out back" fields at the foot of an inactive volcano near the paper mill. I was to have the honor of shooting the first deer. It didn't take long until we picked up the shiny eyes of a very large deer. It looked to weight somewhere around three hundred pounds.

"Shoot him Charlie," the fellow with the light said.

"Bang!" Down he fell.

"Good shot. Sure is a large one."

Well, this is where my getting acquainted with Dr. Jenkins began. That hi-powered gun had a sight scope on it, and I had put my face too close to it when I shot the deer. I had hit the deer, and the scope had hit be on the bridge of my nose. I wiped my face with my hand, and it was very bloody. There was a large cut across my nose.

"Tomorrow is Sunday," one of the fellows said. "Dr. Jenkins is on duty this weekend. You go to his office tomorrow morning, and he will fix you up. We finished our hunting trip and headed home around four am.

I didn't sleep very much that night. Maybe a couple of hours. I went to the doctor about nine the next morning. When I arrived at Dr. Jenkins' office there were about twenty people already waiting. No one was out front. You took a number from a board and waited your turn.

I got my number and took a seat. It wasn't long until I was facing the doctor. Here sat before me a middle-aged man, overweight, wearing short pants and a short-sleeved shirt with a variety of food on the front of it.

"What is the problem?" he asked.

I explained how I cut my nose.

"Sit in that chair," he said. He got up from his chair, put a towel over my eyes, and sprayed something on my nose.

"Tell the next one to come in," he said.

"Doctor, you're not going to sew the gash back together? It will leave a bad scar," I said.

"Are you married?" he asked.

"Yes," I said.

"Well it doesn't matter if you have a scar."

I knew then and there that I might as well get out of his office. I went back to my room and fashioned some small strips from Band-Aids with a pair of nail clippers. I washed the cut and pulled the cut together and held it with the adhesive strips. It healed and didn't leave a scar.

A few weeks later I was invited to a Sunday brunch at one of the local socialite's home. When I arrived, there sat Dr. Jenkins and Minnie, his wife. He was dressed the same as when I first met him, but the food on his shirt was absent. He had got an early start with the booze and was feeling pretty good. I approached him and asked if he would care if I sat with him.

"Fine," he said.

I sat down, and Minnie, his wife and nurse excused herself.

"Dr. Jenkins," I said. "Where did you work before coming to Kawerau?"

He was really friendly and in the mood for talking. He began and told me the following story:

Josh Jenkins was attending lower grade school in Kent. He was not like all the other ten year old boys. He was always reading instead of playing ball or other sports that were played at recess lunchtime. His favorite study was about animals and any other subject about animals and what life is all about. He was destined to become a doctor or a scientist.

Before his fifteenth birthday he had finished all the required subjects in the grade schools. He was now ready to enter medical school at one of the universities, but there was a problem. All the old traditional schools did not want to accept a boy who was so young. He had to convince them that he could keep up with the older students who were in training to become medical doctors.

The board of governors at the University of Birmingham met to decide if admitting him would be wise. They took a vote, and it was decided that he could attend their school. He would start the next semester. Not only did he keep up with the older students, but he was the head of the class in all his studies. He was well on his way to becoming a medical doctor.

By the time his 19th birthday came, he was ready to graduate. He would do his internship at one of the local hospitals, prepare for the medical exam, and open an office to the public. While the other boys his age were living it up and having a good time, Josh had accomplished what he wanted to do. He opened a medical clinic. He had visions of being famous and wealthy, but that didn't seem likely to happen soon. Almost all the people who became sick and needed a doctor were a little afraid to go to a doctor who was so young. In their way of thinking the older the doctor, the more he would know about their problems.

After a year of trying to get his clinic going, Dr. Jenkins decided that he needed to make some changes. He decided that he would join the armed services in the medical corps, get plenty of experience, see the world, and come back some day to open another clinic.

He was in the army medical corps and assigned to the British army hospital in southern India. Little did he know that most of his patients would be the civilians of the small town where the hospital was located. His enlistment was for four years. He could make-out for this short of time and with all the knowledge he would get from experimenting on how to care for the many types of sickness that the Far East people had would be valuable when he returned to civilian practice.

Time passed quickly for Josh because there were always more patients than he could take care of. His four year enlistment was over, and he asked to receive his discharge in India. He had begun to enjoy his working with the native people, and he decided he would start his new clinic in India. He never knew that when he began his practice the Indian government would notify him that the doctors of there worked for them, and that they would be paid a certain amount each month for their services.

This was not what he had expected when he decided to stay in India and continue his doctoring there. He began to make plans for a way out of this situation. He knew that he would have to leave the country to make a change in his practice. He contacted government officials in Burma. They were really pleased to think that they were about to get a very much needed doctor. World War II had just ended and there was a shortage of doctors there in Burma.

They told him that the job was his and that he could begin whenever he wanted to. He wouldn't be working in a hospital or clinic, he was told. There were many small remote villages along the rail route between the Indian border and Rangoon. One of the rail cars was to be his clinic. It would be sort of a moving mini-hospital that would be used to treat and operate on the sick from the many towns and villages along the rail road to and from Rangoon. He would be paid well and supplied with a well qualified nurse to help him take care of the sick. Josh wasn't pleased with the method of payment for his services, but he liked the idea of being on the move all the time. This would fulfill his dream of seeing other places besides the small town where he grew up.

Dr. Jenkins' first trip on his new job was really hectic. He stopped at every village on the rail route from India to Rangoon. He did help a few of the sick, but he soon had filled the rail hospital car to capacity. He would take these patients to the big hospital in Rangoon where they had the most up-to-date equipment available for treating the sick and wounded. Some of Dr. Jenkins's patients died and were beginning to smell. They were giving off an awful odor, and he had to find some way to get rid of them.

The nurse assigned to assist him had served in the army during World War II. She was tough and had an answer for almost anything.

"What shall we do with these corpses?" Dr. Jenkins asked his nurse?

"Well, we can't stop the train and bury them. And besides, there is not enough dry ground along the railroad to dig a grave. It's all jungle with swamps and rivers. And it's full of wild animals and man-eating crocodiles. There's only one thing to do: Have the train stop on the next bridge that crosses a river, and we can throw the dead off the train into the water. They won't last long. The crocks will make short order of them. This will do two things. One, we'll get rid of these stinking dead bodies; and, two, the crocks get a good meal."

Cold chills ran through the doctor's body. He had never heard of such a ruthless act. He soon realized that the nurse was serious and that something had to be done to make room for other patients at the next stop. He sent one of the native orderlies to tell the train engineer to stop on the next bridge so that the medical car would be in the middle of the bridge.

Soon the train stopped and Dr. Jenkins opened the sliding door on the medical car and looked down into the muddy water below. Here he saw many animals including crocodiles.

"Might as well get this over with," he said. He told the nurse to have the orderlies throw the ones that she chose over the side of the bridge. He soon had fifteen fewer patients. The door was closed and the word was sent to the engine crew to begin moving on. He soon reached Rangoon, and all the patients were taken to the local hospital. Several more had died, but they were taken along with the ones who were still alive.

After a few days of rest, he were soon on his way back through the jungle stopping at the many villages along the way. He was beginning to becoming less sensitive toward the sick people he was caring for. The seasoned nurse was teaching him how to treat these poor people of the Burma jungles.

For the next five years Dr. Jenkins made many trips on the train to Rangoon. He had helped many people regain their health and return to their villages. He had also fed the crocodiles and other animals of the jungles along the railroad. He began to tire and decided that he needed to change jobs. His contract with the Burmese government was completed and he had decided that he was not signing another contract to ride the rails back and between Rangoon and India. He began looking around for another assignment.

He was reading the local newspaper at a hotel in Rangoon while resting from his last trip through the jungle. While reading the "help wanted" section, he found this advertisement: "Wanted—medical doctor for general practice in a small town on the North Island of New Zealand. Good pay, vacation, and five eight hour days each week."

"Wow. This is just what I'm looking for," he thought. "I'll be at home every night and have weekends free to do what I want to do; and maybe I'll get married and settle down."

He called the phone number that was in the advertisement. "This is Doctor Josh Jenkins calling about the job in New Zealand. Has the job been taken?"

"No, it's still available. If you would go to the New Zealand embassy in Rangoon and ask for a Mr. Harold Huey, he will give you all the details, and he also has the authority to hire for this job."

"How can anyone be this lucky? Just the thing if I can convince Mr. Huey that I am the one for the job."

Off he went to the embassy to talk with Mr. Huey. He was offered the job and would report for work as soon as he could. The town in New Zeeland where he was going was called Kawerau. It was a small town that was built at the foot of an inactive volcano called Mount Edgecombe. The town was built by a paper manufacturing company for the employees of their new paper mill. It was out in the out-back country. There were several small native Maori villages in the area. Most of the workers at the paper mill were from Europe and Australia.

While working with the veteran nurse on the train, he and she had become good friends. He sort of hated to leave her when going to the new job. He had an idea: why not invite her to come along on this new adventure. Her given name was Minnie,

Minnie Ashcroft. She had been Josh's companion on those many trips through the jungle.

"Minnie," Josh said. "How about quitting this jungle job and coming along with me to New Zealand? I'll tell them that if they want me they will have to give my assistant a job. What do you say?"

"Well, I am sort of getting tired of this kind of life. Been giving some thought to going back to England and working in one of the hospitals. Don't guess it would do any harm to go with you. If I don't like it there, I can always go back to England. It's a deal. I'll come along with you."

Josh was very pleased with this arrangement. Not only was he getting a new job, he was taking a long-time friend and helper with him. And, who knows? Maybe also a good cook and housekeeper.

After quite some time and several more drinks, Dr. Jenkins had given me his version of what a "Burma doctor" was how he had become a doctor in Kawerau, New Zealand.

# Mountain Medicine

The early settlers in the mountains of Western North Carolina did not go to the doctor as we do today for the treatment of sickness. They had their own methods of curing any kind of sickness or injury that they had.

In every settlement in the mountains there was one special person who was considered to have the power to cure every sickness known to these mountain people. This person was usually an older woman, and some people had the idea that this person was a witch who could cast a spell on you and even cause you to die. Just the same, they always sent for her when there was sickness in the family.

The diet of the mountain people was mostly food with a lot of fat. They ate lots of fatback and sow-belly along with any salad greens that were available. In the spring, poke sallet was a favorite along with other leafy greens that grew wild in the fields and along the edges of the woods. The way that they ate was the reason for their number one sickness: stomach problems.

One of their treatments was to wear the root of rhubarb on a string, around the neck. This would prevent stomach cramps. Drinking a tea of hot water poured over the dried lining of the gizzard from a chicken with a little honey added would also cure the stomach ache.

Wild cherry bark made into a tea was used for a cough. Also, sassafras, catnip, horehound, and pennyroyal were boiled and made into a tea for a cough and to treat colds. The leaves from the red cedar were boiled and inhaled for the treatment of bronchitis. Willow tree leaves and bark were made into a tea to break up a fever. Bloodroot, goldenseal, wild ginger, and jack-in-the-pulpit were used for the treatment of many diseases. Resin from the white pine was used for wounds and sores. Powdered bark from the hemlock tree was dried and made into a powder to stop bleeding from a cut. The bark of the hemlock was also good for burns. Cooked pine needles were used for toothache. Rhododendron oil was used for rheumatism. Snake root and dried Indian turnip were made into a tea, sweetened with honey, and used for a variety of aches and pains. These remedies seemed to work, but who would want to get sick and take these medicines? They all tasted awful.

Blood letting was also a common practice used for someone with "too much blood" (high blood pressure). Poultices were used for different ailments. Mustard plasters were used to break up congestion. They would be left on only until the skin began to turn pink. If left on too long, they would blister the skin. Poultices were also made from yellow root and jimson weed, which were plentiful in the summer months.

When someone had the chickenpox, they would be given a nasty tasting tea made from yellow root and Indian turnip. They would drink this awful tasting tea, and within fifteen minutes they would break out, and their fever would come down. If someone had the shingles, you could take the blood of a black chicken, rub it on the area, and they would be cured right away. For warts they notched a willow stick and buried it under the patient's doorstep, or they would rub the wart with a grain of corn and lay in the forks of a road.

Then there was the treatment of the throat disease called "thrash." With thrash, the mouth and throat would be covered with blisters. The only known cure for this was to find someone who had never seen his or her father. This person would blow their breath in the mouth of the one that had the thrash, and he would begin to get better immediately.

If someone had measles and they wouldn't break out, someone would be sent to Mr. Robinson's farm to collect some "sheep pills" (sheep dung). These pills would be wrapped in a thin cloth and then placed in a bowl. Next, they would pour some boiling water over the bag of pills. After they soaked for a few minutes they were removed. A spoon of honey was sometimes added to make the drinking a little easier, and the liquid would be given to the patient. Within an hour the measles would pop out all over the body. Then the patient was on the road to recovery.

When someone got a bad skin rash it was usually referred to as the "itch." The sure cure for this was a good coating of a salve made from sulfur powder and lard that was rendered from the fat of the hog that was killed for winter meat. It usually took several days for the sores to scab over and dry. Given time and patience, this always worked.

Everyone came into contact with poison ivy during the summer months. It was always present on the trees that were in the corn fields and other garden spots. It caused a rash that would drive you crazy by its itching. If you rubbed or scratched the blisters caused by poison ivy, that would make the itching worse. The best treatment was application of a heavy layer of buttermilk mixed with salt. This would stop the itching and start the drying of the blisters.

Head lice were always transferred to your head from someone who had them. For example, if you were sitting at a desk behind someone at school and they had lice, you were pretty sure to get them. How they moved from someone else's head to your head was a mystery. But it happened. The best and sure treatment was to have all the hair removed from your head along with the lice. This was a problem for the girls, so something else had to be done. Sometimes a good combing with a fine toothed "lice comb" followed with a good washing with a strong stinking balm soap that was made with Lysol got rid of the lice. The girls had a much harder time getting rid of them.

Every time someone began to complain with chest pains, the woman of the house would begin to make plans for a good-hot mustard plaster. When this plaster was applied to the chest area, it had to be watched real close so that it didn't make blisters on the skin. It was left on until the skin began to turn pink, then removed. It was supposed to relieve the cramps and pain from the chest area. But it may have been so painful that the patient forgot about the real pain.

Every settler kept several hives of honey bees. This was his main source for sweetening his food. He didn't depend on "store-bought' sugar. With all the bees around everyone was stung sometime or another. The best and sure treatment for a sting was some snuff or tobacco from the mouth rubbed on the sting spot. The treatment was simple because nearly everyone dipped snuff or chewed tobacco.

There were many experts who could get rid of warts on the hands. How these warts were formed no one really knew. We children were told that they came from our handling a toad frog. We did play with frogs sometimes, but I don't think this was the cause. Some wart doctors used a willow stick. They would make notches on the stick for as many warts as you had on your hands. Next they would have you bury it under the doorstep at your house. The number of notches on the stick indicated the number of days before the warts would disappear. Another method was to rub the warts with a greasy dish cloth and not wash your hands for as many days as there were warts. You could also rub a grain of corn on a wart, lay it in the fork of two roads, and the person who picked it up would get your wart.

Believe it or not, many of these methods of doctoring did work, especially those medicines made from roots and berries.

## Medicine Show, 1930s

Believe it or not, there was a lot of entertainment in the mountains and on the farms of Western North Carolina. And a lot of it was free, which was just fine for most all the local people of Canton and Haywood County.

The Medicine Show that came to Canton at least once a year was always a big draw. The Medicine Show was usually a group of four to five people. Of course, the main performer was called the "Doctor" or "The Medicine Man". Some even called him the "Con-Man". Regardless of what we called him, he was a pro. He usually owned the whole outfit, and the others were his employees.

I remember one Medicine Show better than the rest. They came to town and posted notices around town and on trees in the country announcing when and where the show would take place. Everyone had daily chores that had to be done. There was the milking and feeding the hogs, horses, and cows. The notices gave those who were interested time to plan their schedules so they could attend. When the big day arrived, people hustled around and finished their evening chores, ate a quick supper, and hit the road to go see the Medicine Show. The dirty dishes from supper could be washed later.

The stage was already set up, all ready for the show to start. It was on the back of the Medicine Man's truck. The truck was used as a dressing room and to haul all the supplies and entertainers from town to town. Out the Medicine Man came from the back of his truck through the curtains hanging at the back of the stage. The Doc was the star of the show, all dressed up in his black suit and black bowtie.

"Welcome, ladies and gentlemen. Gather up close for some of the best entertainment you will ever see. Tonight we have the best one-man band in this entire country. He plays three musical instruments at a time. Ladies and gentlemen, welcome the one and only, Red Davis!"

Out Red Davis came with his guitar, drums, and harmonica. "What tune do you want him to play?" the Doc asked.

Requests came from every direction.

"Wait a minute," Doc said. "Red can play any tune you want, but he can't play them all at the same time. Tell you what, how about "Orange Blossom Special"?

Old Red was already playing, and some were clapping their hands and humming along. Doc was just getting the crowd in the mood for the real show.

Old Red played several songs on his instruments and sang one. He played his songs regardless of what the crowd asked for. When Old Red was finished warming up the crowd, he left his drums on the stage and went back into the truck. The curtains were hardly closed before a pretty young lady jumped out, dressed in brightly colored clothes with a blouse that left her belly bare and a short skirt nearly up to her knees. All the men folk stretched their necks and tried to get up closer. Many got a good elbow in the ribs from their wives.

"What I have to offer you tonight is one of the modern miracles of medicine. You children move back so mom and dad can get up close! Yes sir, this is the best medicine on the market today. When you buy from me, you have a 100% guarantee that it will do everything I say it will do."

"How many of you folks have aching backs, arms, legs, and other pains? How about that tired feeling after a hard day's work or a nagging headache? Folks, I have the answer to all your problems right here."

He turned to the young lady and said, "Mother would you hand me a couple of bottles of 'Chief Running Deer's Secret'? This medicine is made from roots, bark, and other secret ingredients straight from the woods of the Cherokee Indian Reservation. I am the only white man allowed to sell it. You children move back, let the grown folks come up close."

"My price for this miracle medicine is only fifty cents a bottle. But if you want to have a good supply for the winter, I will let you have three for a dollar. Friends, I will probably lose money, but I want to take a vacation and need to sell it all! You, my lucky friends, get a bargain. Red, Mother, and I are leaving in a few days. Better hurry! What I have will go fast, and there ain't no more outside the Cherokee Nation."

Out came a dollar from my mom's apron pocket. She handed it to Doc. "Mother, hand this fine lady three bottles of that miracle medicine. Who's next?"

There were hands everywhere with a dollar in them. Doc and his young assistant were really busy. The ones who bought the tonic headed toward home. Soon everyone was gone, and Doc and his crew started to pack everything into the truck. After a very good night, they were ready to move on.

When we arrived home, Mom had to wash the dishes that we left on the table hurrying to the Medicine Show. Mom hadn't been in the kitchen very long until she started singing. She usually hummed or sang when she was working, but this time she was really letting it come out.

"WHEN THE SAINTS GO MARCHING IN. WHEN THE... SAINTS GO..."

"Mom? What's wrong with you?"

"Oh, I was pretty tired and had an aching back, so I took a good dose of the medicine. WILL THERE BE ANY STARS...."

Mom was letting the music out, LOUD AND CLEAR. Dad went to the kitchen and asked Mom if he could see the medicine.

He looked on the back of the bottle where the ingredients were listed: "50 % alcohol— 50 % spring water— Artificial coloring and flavoring— Patent applied for."

Now Dad was known to like a good drink of homemade whiskey ever so often. "Wonder if Doc has left yet? I need a few bottles of that medicine. Can't ever tell when I'll get sick. Better hurry before he gets to the next county." And off he went.

Mom's singing was becoming louder. "THIS LITTLE LIGHT OF MINE…" Mom was feeling her best. That medicine really did work.

Next year there would be another "Medicine Show" coming to Canton but usually had a different Medicine Man. We didn't care who came. The entertainment was always good, and it was always free. Also, the medicine seemed to help the "sick" people. Hope he doesn't stay away too long.

# Gone Hunting, 1936

Tomorrow is the big day. "I'd better go to bed early if I am to get an early start. I've got to leave early if I'm going all the way to the watershed on Beaverdam Mountain."

My plan for tomorrow was to go hunting in the watershed that was located on the Beaverdam side of Little Sam Mountain in the Thickety section of Haywood County, North Carolina. I got up at 4 AM and had a quick breakfast of cornbread that was left from last night's supper along with a big glass of milk. This was fine. It was too early for Mom to get up and cook. If she did, this would take time, and I had to get going.

My gun and hunting coat were ready, and so was I. I put the coat on and checked to make sure that my belt was full of shotgun shells. Didn't want to be short of shells for my old 12 gauge shotgun.

It was getting close to 4:30, and I was on my way. It was still dark, but I had traveled the road toward Little Sam many times, and I didn't have any trouble finding my way.

I was soon at the foot of the mountain and taking the shortcut through the woods instead of going along the road. The curve was very long because the mountain was very steep, and the curve was one of several before reaching the top.

I had walked about half of the shortcut when I stopped to rest for a minute. I was leaning against a big tree when I suddenly heard a strange noise above in the tree. I began to look around to see what was going on. The dawn was beginning to break and the sky was getting a little lighter. There it was again—the noise was coming from some kind of animal or bird at the top of the tree. I could see it moving a little. I pulled the hammer back on my gun, raising it up and pointing toward whatever that was in the tree.

"BANG!" Down it came. I quickly put another shell in the gun and moved toward whatever it was that I had shot. I moved it with the toe of my shoe to see if it was dead. It didn't move any, so I picked it up. Right away I knew what I had killed. It was a big rooster. Not the ordinary chicken rooster but a big pheasant rooster.

At first I was real proud, and then I began to think. What if the Game Warden checks to see what I have in my coat pocket? The season for hunting pheasants was not open; only the squirrel season was open. I hurried on my way hoping that I didn't meet anyone.

I was soon at the top of the mountain in what was called Crabtree Gap. I would take the sled road going to the right on the top of the mountain. This road was for a horse drawn sled or walking only. I was on my way to the watershed. This was where the water for the town of Canton came from. It was a large fenced-in area where no hunting was permitted. This is was what made the hunting more exciting, doing what you were not supposed to do, and the game was plentiful inside that fence.

I killed a couple of squirrels alongside the road on my way. Soon a log house came into sight. It wasn't far from the fence around the water shed. As I came closer I could see several small children playing some sort of game in front of the house. They were all bare-footed; no shoes on their feet. When they saw me they began to vanish. Soon the yard was empty.

I was near the house when a man in a faded pair of overalls came out. He looked as though he hadn't shaved for a week or so. He put out his hand and said, "My name is Bill Overman. My old lady and our five kids live here. Welcome to the Overman home."

"Glad to meet you," I said. "I live down the mountain in the Thickety section of Canton. My name is Fletcher, and I am out squirrel hunting."

"Had any luck?" he asked.

"I killed a couple of squirrels and a bird on my way up the mountain." I put my hand in my coat pocket and pulled out the bird and handed it to him.

"WOW!" he said. "Sure is a big bird. 'Bout as big as I've seen lately."

I pulled out the two squirrels and handed them to him. "You can have the rooster and the squirrels. I'll kill me a mess on my way back down the mountain."

"Hate to take your meat, but I thank ye. Was wondering what we would have for dinner. The old lady had better get busy getting them ready to cook."

He left me standing alone and went into the house and returned within a minute. "Got her started, won't be long until they will be on the fire."

As we were talking, the children began to come from I don't know where. There were three small girls and two boys. The boys were older than the girls, but I would guess that the eldest was somewhere around twelve. All of them had the minimum of clothes on. It was early fall and a little chilly, but they didn't seem to mind the weather. They were mountain people and knew how to get by with the bare minimum of everything.

"I'll be back by in a little while," I said. "I'm going into the watershed and see if I can find a few squirrels."

"You ought to find a lot over there. The last time I was there, the hickory trees were loaded with nuts. Ain't nothing that a squirrel likes more than a hickory nut. Be sure and stop by on your way back."

I crossed the fence and soon found a hickory grove of about five trees. This was a good place to sit and wait. I was there for over an hour and never saw the first squirrel, must have been too late in the day. I did see a gray fox down in the hollow. He never saw me because he was trotting slowly around the mountainside.

I soon called it quits and returned to the Overman house. Bill was in the yard as if he was expecting me. "Any luck," he asked.

"No," I said. "They've all eat a big breakfast and are laying around sleeping. Got to get down the mountain anyway. The sun will be going down soon."

"The old lady has dinner ready and you better eat before leaving. Got plenty for everyone. Come on in."

I was a little hungry, and I also knew that if you were invited to eat with these mountain people and refused, it made them feel bad. It was a custom to accept their invitation for a meal.

We went into the house. There was a long table made from wide boards along with matching benches on both sides. Bill found two chairs somewhere and placed one at each end of the table. "You set at that end, and I'll set at the other," he said.

The food was already on the table. After a short blessing prayer, Bill picked up the plate with the cooked pheasant. "Ain't no one who can cook like my old lady. She salted and peppered this bird and then rolled it in flour. Here, get yourself a piece."

I took a leg and passed the plate back to him. He took a piece and handed the plate to his wife. She divided what was left with the children and didn't have any left for herself. Next came the big pot of squirrel and dumplings. I was served first and then the others. Next was the plate of corn pones. What a dinner. Everything was delicious.

I looked around for a cook stove but didn't locate one. I did see iron rods with hooks on the end in the big fireplace. I am sure that is where this meal was cooked.

I got my coat and gun and was leaving when Bill said, "If you are ever this way again, stop by and set a spell. You are always welcome."

I returned the invitation to him and his family. He said, "you know, we don't go to Canton very often. Only when we need snuff, tobacco, or sugar. We don't have much money. I sell a few animal hides in the winter. When I have more pigs than I need, I take them down the mountain and sell them. We have everything here on the mountain. A mule, a cow, chickens, and several hogs. The animals feed themselves in the pasture and woods. We have a big garden, and the old lady cans for the winter food. The 'Good Lord' takes care of us."

We shook hands, and I left for my trip back home. I had met and made a new friend. In my long life I have gone hunting many times, but never have I experienced anything like the trip to the watershed, the Overman house, the meal, and the lesson I learned from the lifestyle of this mountain family. I can truly say that I have gone hunting.

# Fishing Trip

When growing up I didn't have many opportunities to go fishing. That is, "real" fishing. Where we lived there were no fish in the nearby Pigeon River below the paper mill. My brother and I would fish in the creeks, but we only caught small fish and sometimes a crawfish. We didn't have any fishing equipment except the hooks we made from safety pins, line made from the string from Mom's sewing box and a fishing pole made from the straightest limb we could find from a tree.

With our hand-made fishing gear, a big can of red worms, and a couple of biscuit and country ham sandwiches that were left from breakfast we were on our way to one of the many creeks for some serious fishing. It didn't bother us about what we would catch or how large it was, we were having a good time trying to outsmart whatever tried to make a meal of the worm on the hook. The fish that we caught were small honey head or large branch minnows that we called "silversides." None were ever over three or four inches long. It didn't make any difference; we were fishing.

When we were finished fishing, we gathered our fishing "tackle" together and headed toward home. We didn't have any fish, but we had fun trying to catch them. As we walked along we made plans for another day of fishing at another creek.

When we visited our uncles who lived up the river above the paper mill, they would sometimes take us to the "big fishing hole" in the bend of the river. The fish that we caught here were larger, and there were several different types. There were hog sucker, horney head, red horse, perch, silverside; and every once in a while we would catch a native trout that had wandered from the many trout streams on the mountain. There was an alligator-like "lizard" that was sometimes 10 or 12 inches long but didn't have teeth and didn't try to bite you. We were afraid of them, but we did catch one every so often. When Uncle Bob took us fishing, Aunt Roxie came along. We would usually catch enough for a small "fish fry" when we returned home. The fish we caught were very bony, and we had to be careful not to swallow any bones when we ate them.

There was an "old folk's tale" about drinking milk with fish. It was said that this combination was poison and could kill you. This was fine with me because Aunt Cory always had a big pitcher of some kind of drink she made from her secret ingredients to go along with the fish. She wouldn't tell you what it was. She referred to it as "beer". I guess that she never passed her recipe along to anyone. These mountain people had their secrets and seldom gave them away.

I got to fish in the big lake at the Methodist Church Assembly called Lake Junaluska a couple of times. The fish were bigger there, and there were lots of them. The prize fish that everyone tried to catch was the carp. We would make bait for carp by mixing flour with cotton. We made what we called "dough balls." This was the type of bait that everyone used when trying carp. Not only were they large fish, but they were a good eating fish.

I guess that I inherited the love for hunting and fishing from my dad. He did a lot of hunting and fishing when we were growing up. He would sometimes take me along on a few hunting trips but never on one of his overnight fishing trips.

One evening he came home from his job at the paper mill and said, "I don't have to work this Saturday. I think I'll go night fishing. You boys can come along if you want to. Better dig some worms for bait for tomorrow. I'll get some chicken liver for the cat fish. Get everything ready that you think you will need. We will leave as soon as I get home."

He then began to tell Mom what pots and pans and food we would need to take along. Things got exciting after that for me; I had never been on a real fishing trip. Dad said that we were going to Whittier and fish in the Tuckasegee River. John Styles was going with us. He was born and raised in that area. He knew all the locations of the best fishing holes. He was also one of Dad's "good time" buddies, and TJ and I knew that there would be some drinking of "white lighting" on this fishing trip. This didn't bother us at all as long as we were going on a big fishing trip, camping out on the river bank, exploring the area, and maybe even doing some fishing.

I don't know how the Tuckasegee River got its name. The Cherokee Indians believed that a large sea-type monster lived in this river, and they avoided it as much as possible. The word "Cherokee" means "People of the Mountains," and "Tuckasegee" probably has a meaning in the Cherokee language, too.

The big moment had arrived when Dad came from the paper mill. Everything was packed and sitting on the porch waiting to be put into the car. "You boys carry everything to the car, and I will load it into the car. Got to leave room for John. I'll pick him up at his house. We will still need room for his fishing gear and whatever food he has to take along. Better get going. It will be a long time until dark. The daylight is here longer in the summer. We have to cook supper before we start fishing. If someone didn't leave some wood we will have to get some for the fire."

After a few more comments and instructions, we were in the car and on our way to an unknown part of the world. Although Dad had been to many parts of the country, TJ and I had not been too far from our home.

We stopped at John's house, and he loaded his stuff in the car. We were soon on the main road, US Route 19/23 headed towards

Whittier and the river. TJ and I were not missing a thing as we were in a part of the world that we had never seen before. The road across Balsam Mountains was beautiful. Once at the top you could see for miles across the tall spruce, balsams, and many other types of trees, even a few chestnuts every now and then. There were many small streams coming down the mountainsides from the springs that came from under a rock cliff or some big tree. As they joined each other they became larger streams that had the native trout fish in them. Soon we were in the bottomlands and following the river that we were to fish in. Dad pulled the car off the road into a flat space on the riverbank.

"Here we are" Jack said.

"Where is the town of Whittier?" I asked.

"Straight across the river," Jack said.

"I don't see any houses or stores over there," I said.

"See that swinging bridge down there?" Jack said. "There are several houses over there. You don't see them because they are up in the hollows and coves. The people use the footbridge to get across the river. If they have their wagons loaded with corn to take to the corn mill to have it ground, they go down the river a little ways and cross where the water is only about a foot deep. This is called, "forging the river." You can also wade across if you watch out for slick rocks. If you step on one you are sure to fall and get wet all over."

Everything for our camp was set. Jack had built a fire, and Dad was getting the pans out to start our supper meal before dark. TJ and I decided to look around a little. There was plenty of wood for the fire, so we were free to do what we wanted to do. We went straight to the swinging bridge. We had never seen anything like this before. We decided to cross the river on the bridge. When we were near the middle, the whole bridge began to swing back and forth. We held tight to the cables on the sides and were soon on the other bank of the river.

We had begun to explore the bank of the river when I spotted something moving in the water on the edge of the bank. I got closer to get a better look, and I saw a great big fish with a string in its mouth. I got closer and, low and behold, that fish was caught on a "bank fishing" line.

"Let's take him and to show Dad and Jack what we caught," I said. "Yeah," TJ said.

I untied the line from a small bush and pulled the fish out onto the bank and into the grass. "Sure is a big one," I said. "I don't think I can carry him by myself."

We looked around and found a tree limb that was pretty straight and about four feet long. We tied the line in the middle, and with TJ on one end and me on the other, we went back across the bridge. We were so excited that we didn't notice the bridge swinging.

As we approached the fishing place we began to holler, "Look what we caught!"

Jack and Dad looked around, and one of them said, "My God! Look at that! Biggest catfish I've ever seen. Must be five or six pound."

They both picked the fish up and took a good look at him. "I'll get my knife and a pair of pliers and skin that booger. We'll have fish for supper tonight."

Jack began the job of dressing the fish as though he had dressed a cat fish before. It didn't take him long until there was a big pan full of fish ready to be cooked. Dad put a big cast iron frying pan on the fire, put some of the lard shortening he brought along in the pan, and pretty soon there was a full pan of fish getting ready for our supper.

After turning the fish a few times so they were brown on all sides ,Dad said, "Jack, get the pork and beans open and some bread from the box in the back seat of the car. And get some of the paper plates. We are ready to eat."

And eat we did. There was enough fish for everyone with a couple of pieces left over. "Bout the best fish meal I ever had," Jack said.

"Me too," Dad said. Better get things cleaned up. Won't be long before it's dark, and all the light we have is that kerosene lantern we brought for light to fish by tonight."

It wasn't long until everything was put in its proper place and we were all fishing. "Where are we going to sleep?" I asked Dad.

"We aren't," he said. "We come to catch some fish, not to sleep."

I didn't say anything. I was looking around for a good grassy place near the fire. I had never stayed awake all night before and didn't plan on starting now.

Everything went well. We had caught a few fish of different kinds but nothing as big as our cat fish. About what I thought was midnight everything became quiet. Dad and Jack had been sampling their "moonshine" and were getting sleepy. TJ and I were also ready to find a good place to curl up for the rest of the night. We found a place where the grass was thick, and we lay down. We didn't need anything to cover ourselves because it was mid-summer and very warm. It was not long until everyone was still. Jack and Dad had also found a sleeping place.

We were awakened the next morning when someone hollowed, "Get up. The fish are biting, and you all are asleep. Get up. The day's half gone."

I rubbed my eyes to get a better look at our visitors. There stood two men who looked like they hadn't shaved or had a bath for several weeks (or months). Dad was now awake and he asked, "What are you fellows doing here?"

"We come to do a little fishing. This is the best fishing hole on this river. You fellers don't care if we join you, do you?"

"No," Dad said. There's room for everybody."

Soon, everyone was around the fire where dad was frying some ham and eggs for our breakfast. "You fellers hungry? he asked our visitors.

"Wouldn't hurt none if we did have a bite."

"I'll cook a couple more eggs, then, and you can eat with us."

Soon breakfast was over. "We are much obliged for the good breakfast," one of the men said.

"Glad to have you," Dad said.

A little later we were all fishing when we had another visitor drop by. "Howdy," he said. "Catching anything?"

"One every once in a while," Jack said.

"I'm the game warden in this county. My name is Bob Henderson. You may have heard of me. Everyone in this county says that I'm the best warden they ever had. I ketch a lot of 'outsiders' who come here to fish. Can I see your fishing licenses?"

TJ and I didn't have to have a license because we were under twelve years old. Dad and Jack showed him their licenses.

"How about you fellers? he said to the other men.

"Ain't got any. Never had any and never will. It's a shame you government people are always after more money from us working people. Go away and leave us be."

"I'll have to take you to jail if you don't have a license. Come on, I'm taking you in."

You ain't taking us anywhere, so you may as well get going."

"I'll go get some help and be back. Both of you will be in jail before the sun goes down today. I'll be back with plenty of help. You stay right here."

"You get all the help you want. We ain't going anywhere. We ain't got no money to buy a license and wouldn't if we did. They tell me that you get a dollar for every body you catch. I may get me some of that government money as soon as I get my corn laid by. Got nearly two acres planted this year. Yes sir, sure keeps me busy on that farm. I may get me one of them government jobs this fall. I hear that they are hiring for work on the WPA. Pays real good money, they say. Something like one or two dollars a day. Seems the government has lots of money."

It was easy to see that our new-found friends had been drinking before they came to do some fishing.

"You fellers have anything to drink," they asked?

"We have a little left," Jack said. You can have a little drink but leave some for us."

He passed the half gallon jar to one of them. The man had a drink and handed the jar to the other man. He also took a drink and handed it back to Jack. "Guess we better be going before that law man comes back. Thank you for the eats and the drink. If you fellers are ever back this way, stop and pay us a visit. We live on the other side of the river about two miles down. Better go now."

Along in the evening the warden came back. He had two pretty big men with him. "Where are they?" he asked.

Dad spoke up: "They said they got tired of waiting for you to come back, so they left. Said they were going home, wherever that is. You might catch up with them. They went up the road toward Sylva. They left without saying anything else."

It was getting up in the afternoon and we were tired of fishing, so we began to pack for the trip back home to Canton. We were soon on our way. TJ and I were tired, but we weren't sorry we went on this trip. We had caught some fish in addition to the big cat fish, had some good eating, and met two local strangers who seemed to be living the life that many of the mountain people of Western North Carolina lived. We had been on a real fishing trip, but for the rest of the summer we would have to do our fishing on the creek bank.

# Prayer Meeting

Every now and then you hear an older person say, "You should have seen or you should have had to do so-and-so or such-and-such in the good old days." I grew up in what is sometimes referred to as the "good old days." At times the good old days were not that good. The effects of the great depression had something to do with the way we did things everyday.

Not only was the workplace affected by the "hard luck times," the way we worshiped and carried on our loyalty to our church and God had changed, too. A church and the leadership of an ordained minister weren't always available. The building that we called the church was always there, but the minister had a family to feed and clothe and had to work, or he had other churches to pastor and had to schedule services so everyone would have a pastor at least once in a while.

However, the worship services never stopped. They were carried on by having what we called "Prayer Meeting". The faithful of the church would gather at someone's house at least once every week. There would be singing, reading from the Bible, praying, and lots of testifying and shouting. The church member's house that was used changed with each meeting.

I was not a teenager at this time, but I had to attend most of the meetings with my Mom. She was a very religious person and she attended all of these meetings if she possibly could. And guess who was always with her? Me, the oldest child in our family. Mom could never get Dad to go with her. He always had an excuse and sometimes said, "Ellen, (Mom's name), you have enough religion for the both of us."

There was one house where the meetings were held that I liked to go to. This was the home of the lady who played the organ at Oak Grove Church where Mom went, usually taking me, my brother, and the two girls, my sisters. It was Aunt Molly Anderson's house. The largest crowd would always be there. I guess it was because Aunt Molly had a pump organ, and there was more singing here than at the other places we met. She would pump and play that organ so loud that windows would rattle. Also, she had the loudest voice of all the singers. I loved to hear her play, but after a few meetings, I do believe that whatever the song was, the music always sounded the same. But she did make a "joyful noise."

One prayer meeting that I will never forget was held at our house. We were living in a section of Canton that was called Mingus Cove. We had a fairly large house at the time. As was the case with a lot of the buildings in the mountains of Western North Carolina, it had a high side off the ground. After all, there were not many level places. Most houses were on hillside.

Well, the side of our house near the narrow dirt road was sitting on wooden posts about four feet off the ground. This was a common for a foundation. Some people used field stone instead of wood.

The night of the meeting Mom sent us to bed early so there would be more room for the adults attending the meeting. Soon there were about twelve people in the living room of our house. The meeting started after the usual handshakes and hugs. Someone was chosen to lead the singing. There was no musical instrument, and the singing was loud and way off-key.

There was a prayer, and then the testimonies started. This was when the shouting, "amens," and arm waving began. Soon everyone was happy and "praising the Lord." The house began to shake a little, and then, without warning, one corner of the house fell toward the ground. It dropped about three feet. The bedroom where we children were was on the corner that fell. Our beds moved from one wall to the lower side of the room. Out of the beds came four scared children.

We ran into the parlor with the prayer meeting crowd. Well now, times were hard, and very few people wore pajamas. All of the poor people slept in their underclothes This was the way the prayer people saw us, in our underclothes. Most everyone was trying to get out of the house. One of the men hollered, "Let the women out first. Amen! Hallelujah!" I don't think anyone saw the four children trying to get out of the house. It was everyone for himself. Everyone quickly got out of the house and went their separate ways home.

Mom stood staring at us kids. "I think it'll be all right to go back to bed," she said. "Your dad will be home soon, and he will take a look and see what happened."

So, we got back into the beds that seemed like they were on their ends.

The next morning two of the men who were at the meeting when the house fell down came around. "We come over to help raise the house up," they said. Dad had gone to work in the paper mill, so these two me were going to set things right.

After looking at the problem, they left. Soon they came back with a jack, a long wooden pole, and a short one with a fork on one end (where two limbs joined together). The short pole was the "heel." The long pole was the lever for doing the lifting.

After several jackings and lifts with the poles, they had the house back on the corner post that it was sitting on before the prayer meeting. "I think that will hold it," one of the men said. Mom thanked them, and they left.

There were many more prayer meetings after this one, but I do not remember having another one at our house.

# Full-time Preacher

The first time that I can recall seeing and hearing a preacher was at a "brush arbor" meeting. The men of the community built this meeting shelter for the soon to be held "old fashioned revival meeting." The preacher would be the same one who was there a year ago. His schedule was pretty much the same every year unless the meeting was going real well and the elders of the community would have him stay an extra week. This didn't happen very often, only when the area that he was at was having some kind of troubles in the community that needed that extra blessing from the Lord.

This meeting shelter was built from small trees called saplings. Posts were placed in the ground to form the outside walls. Then longer poles were tied across the top. These were to hold the leafy tree branches that would be the roof of the meeting place. This gave good protection from the sun but was not the best shelter from the rain, although it did keep you from getting wet if it was only a short shower. But if it was a really heavy rain for a long period of time, you could expect to get a good soaking. Most everyone didn't mind though. After all, we only had these meetings once a year.

These brush arbor meetings were where everyone confessed all the bad things that they had done since the last meeting. This was a time to ask to be forgiven and a time to turn over a new leaf for the upcoming year.

Not only was there preaching every night, but there was something for all the children during the day. The preacher, with some help from the mothers, would have contests for the girls and the boys. The children were divided into teams according to ages, and sometimes the winning teams received small prizes. Although the boys tried really hard to show the girls who were the smartest, the girls usually won the contests.

All the contests were based on the Bible. We all learned a lot from these games. I could quote from the old and new books of the Bible and knew whole pieces of the Bible such as the 23rd. Psalm. After 80 years, I still remember lots of the things we were taught at these revival meetings. I guess this was our "Bible School" of the 20s and 30s.

These meetings also had a few other benefits for the old and the young. The adults cut back their work to a minimum, and the young got out of a lot of chores that they had to do everyday. I guess this accounted for the good attendance of the "Day School" at the arbor. These meetings also provided lots of good eating that we ordinary didn't get. These preachers were well feed. They were paid very little because no one had any money during the depression of the 1930s. The preacher would get a few dollars and a "pounding" before he left. But he did get good meals everyday, and all the meals usually had southern fried chicken as a main dish. It was a well known fact that everybody's chicken flock was a lot smaller after the preacher left. No one begrudged this, and everyone looked forward to these visits from the "Circuit Riding" preacher.

On September the 2nd, 1899, a small group of Baptists met to organize a church in the Thickety Township of Haywood County, North Carolina. This group had their first meetings in Cabe's Chapel School House. The first name for this church was New Hope Baptist Church. In February 1901, a preacher by the name of James Ruben Liner led the small group to build a permanent church. There were two other known preachers who followed James Liner after the building of the first church.

They were Mont Haynes and M. Caldwell.

We moved to the Thickety community in the 1930s. At the time the community had a building set aside specially for church services. This church was called Oak Grove Baptist Church. Oak Grove Church has served many generations over the past 100 plus years. The church got its name from the many oak trees in the grove where it was built. The church building that is used today was also built close by. There were many large oak trees where the building is now, but they were removed to make way for the present building.

I have had many thoughts of these trees throughout my life, the reason being that our contribution to building the present structure was for our family to dig out these trees. There was no digging equipment such as bulldozers and backhoes, so all the digging was by pick and shovel. This was slow and a lot of hard work. Guess who the most of this digging was assigned to? None other than TJ, my younger brother, and me. Dad was working in the paper mill, and he would help out some only when he was home.

We didn't have too much trouble with the smaller trees, but there was one that was about four feet in diameter and its main roots grew straight down. We dug for several days and were deep enough that we couldn't see out when in the hole around the tree. Dad gave it a look and came up with the idea that it would have to be blasted out.

One of his buddies who lived close by, Dink Wines, had been blowing out some stumps on his dad's farm, and he volunteered to blast out our last tree. It was all set for one evening when Dad came home from the paper mill. Dink met us at the tree. He brought two sticks of dynamite, some fuse, and blasting caps. TJ and I were all excited.

Dink looked the tree over and decided that it would only take one stick of dynamite to do the job. He placed it where he figured it would have the best effect. After the blast, we all ran to see how big of a hole had been made. We saw that our last tree had indeed been dug up.

Dink and Dad rolled themselves a cigarette from their sack of "Golden Grain" tobacco. We all were sitting in the hole where the tree had been. It so happened that this area was known to be a place where boys brought their girlfriends. I suppose it was because there were no houses within a mile, and they wanted privacy. About then a car drove up with two boys and their girlfriends. They parked across the road where the old schoolhouse used to be. Then the couples went in different directions.

Dink spoke up: "Let's have some fun with these young people. We still have one stick of dynamite left. I'll cut it in half. You take one half, and I'll take the other. You go down the road on that side of the woods, and I'll go on the other side. Look at your watch, and I'll look at mine. At 6:35 we'll both light our fuses."

TJ and I were down in the tree hole when the first BAM went off. A couple of seconds later there was another BAM. Then out came one of the boys and his girl, and into the car they got. They started their engine and started to leave. They only were a little ways away when here came the other couple. "Wait for us," they were hollering. Finally they got to the car that was quite aways down the road. Digging the trees was finally some fun instead of all work.

The area now cleared of trees, it was time for the Sorrels, Harrises, Willises, Tathems, McClearys, and all the other people of the community to bring their horses, mules, plows, and dirt scoops. The basement had to be dug. Here again TJ and I volunteered.

It was not all long hours and hard work. At dinner time, (lunch) the women would bring all the workers something to eat. It was something special every day. I do think the women folks tried to outdo each other. This we didn't mind and said nothing that would change the good food we were getting.

After several weeks of plowing, digging with a mattock, and moving tons of dirt and stone, we had the perfect hole in the ground for the basement that would be the Sunday School rooms when the building was finished. Everyone was proud of the part they had in getting this far, but there was a long way to go to get our new, modern church.

The first thing was to find someone to oversee the building. Some of the men in the neighborhood were what you could call "jack leg" carpenters. They could build a hog pen or a barn but were not about to try to build the building that we wanted. We needed an experienced building supervisor.

Soon the perfect person was hired to oversee the building. His name was John Buchanan. He was a well-known builder from the eastern part of the state. He only had one leg. How he had lost his leg no one ever knew, nor did they ask him. He couldn't do any climbing but he could tell anyone what to do and how, and it was always right.

Soon the building began to take shape. Mountain stone was used to make the walls of the basement. Then the wood framing, the floor, the roof and went up, and there was the rough part of the new church building. It was decided that the outside walls were to be brick so the building would last a long time and this work wouldn't have to be repeated in the next few years. The elders of our community were planning for the future of their children's children and their families.

I was a helper in this, and to this day I still remember the way John Buchanan went about his work. Good was not enough. Everything had to be perfect. I learned a lot from this man.

Soon the finishing touches were done, and we were ready to have our first services in our new building. This had to be a very special day for everyone who lived in the Thickety community whether they were Baptist or Methodist. Everyone was invited to come and celebrate this modern "House of the Lord". They did come. Some in wagons, some walking, others in cars or trucks. The women had been cooking and preparing for this special day for the full week before, and there was plenty of good food along with the all day preaching and singing. The small children would have the time of their life playing many games with each other. This was one big happy family. They were proud of this new Church.

I left the Thickety community in the early 40s when the war started and returned in 1946. I married one of the long-time members of this Church. Marie had attended Oak Grove since she was a small girl. We both became members of the church and were active in their services until 1953 when we moved away. I had accepted employment with a paper mill in Tennessee.

Upon moving to Cleveland, Tennessee, one of our first things in getting settled in our new home was locating a church to attend. We didn't have to look very far before we decided that North Cleveland Baptist Church was where we would move our membership. I learned later that this church was started from a brush arbor many years ago. The church building that was here when we joined in 1953 was a small white wooden building. There was no air conditioning, and the heating was a big coal burning heater. It was simple but very friendly and sincere about the Lord's work. The first full time preacher was Reverend McDonald. It was a good group of people just like the ones we had left at Oak Grove Baptist in North Carolina. North Cleveland Baptist would be our new church home.

Many years have passed since leaving our church in North Carolina and joining North Cleveland Baptist here in Tennessee and many building and remolding projects have taken place at both churches. The Oak Grove Church has added additional rooms for Sunday School and also built a house for Reverend

Bruce Clayton, who has been the pastor of this Church for over 26 years. The church has been blessed from his leadership.

North Cleveland Baptist has also grown over the many years from its beginning. We now have a large sanctuary that seats about 300 people, a two story education building with class rooms, offices for the staff personnel, a small kitchen, and restrooms. We also have an annex with a fellowship room complete with a modern kitchen along with a library and classrooms for the older people of the Church. The senior pastor is Dr. Jay McCluskey who has lead the church for over 21 years. The church has grown so fast under his leadership that he has one full-time and two part time assistants. They are all ordained Baptist preachers. There are plans to do some additional building to accommodate the needs of the church.

The only two Churches that I have belonged to have a similar history. They both started from a temporary meeting place and have grown over the many years. I keep informed through my relatives and friends about the happenings and latest news from my old home place. I recently received a phone call from Neil Clark. He was asking about his Dad who I grew up with. I had forgotten Neil. The last time I saw him he was a small child. He told me that he was now teaching the older senior Sunday School class at Oak Grove. This would be the ones around my age (80 plus). This is a good indication that this church will be there for many more years.

Many years have passed since I went off to war and returned to dedicate my life to the Lord, join Oak Grove Church, move to Tennessee, join North Cleveland church, and watch both churches grow. There is one thing in common between these two churches: They both started from a humble beginning, with a part time preacher, and a dedicated group of Christians who had a vision for the future. Their prayers were answered: They now had a full-time preacher.

# The Radio

It is likely that the younger generation has no knowledge of where we heard our favorite music and the popular shows of the 1930s. It was the battery powered "RADIO."

Only a few homes in the mountains of Western North Carolina had a radio. They had no money to buy anything but the necessary things to feed and clothe their family. It was the great depression years of the 30s.

Our home was located in the Beaverdam section of Haywood County, North Carolina. It was located at the foot of the mountains and the family that owned one of these battery powered radios lived about a three mile walk up the mountain. This route was the only way to reach his house. A foot trail winding around the mountain side.

The family went by the name of Scott. Like all homes in the early days of our country, all families were large and the Scott home had many children. They were like most every one else in these mountains. The were neighbors and

Everyone was welcome in their home,

Having the only radio in the area made their home a very popular place most every evening. My brother, TJ and I would hurry home from school, get all of our assigned jobs done, feeding the hogs, milking the cow and cut the wood for the fireplace and cook stove for the next day. We would hurry through our school home work and head out for the Scott home.

When we arrived, Mr. Scott would already be at his station by the radio. He owned the radio and was the official operator.

No one else was allowed to touch the dials. We listened to what he wanted to hear, no questions asked.

With the help of about 100 ft. of wire strung through the trees he could usually get two stations, sometimes three. The most popular programs were Lum and Abner and the other that started off with the blood curdling screeching of a door opening. This was a continue story and a very good mystery.

Lum Edwards and Banner Peabody were the two old fellows that operated the Jot-Em-Down store. The setting was in the small town of Pine Ridge Arkansas. Lum was a bachelor and was always after the widow Abernathy. Abner kept the store going and Cedric WeHunt was always trying to help Lum get the widow Abernathy to notice him. They were always fussing and dividing the store between them.

The big shot in town was Squire Skimp who had the answers for everything that needed fixing. This was a very funny show and kept the attention of the whole crowd.

Amos and Andy was about two Africa-Americans and were sort of like Lum and Abner. The actors for the show were Charles Corell and Freeman Gosden, they were white. Amos was the bachelor of the show and all the women were after him. Most of the shows were continued so that you would be left wandering what would happen the next night. We could hardly wait for the next show to see if Madam Queen would marry Andy. We were hooked on these radio programs

The program that everyone liked was on every Saturday night. You had to have a pretty long aerial wire to receive this program because of the distance of the broadcasting station was quit a distance from our area. It was the radio station WSM located in Nashville, Tennessee. It was called "The Grand Old Opry". It would start at 7 PM and end at 12 PM. The entire program was Bluegrass and Country music with a little country comedy every now and then. Only the best of the country artists were on this show. There was an African American on the show but his race was never mentioned because of the segregation in the South. His name would be given and the music he would play. His name was De-Ford Bailey and he was a master harmonica player. He was my hero and I tried to copy his style of playing for many years.

Back at home about 9 PM when the music was fast and loud it was common for some one to hit the floor dancing to the music, The dance was mostly clogging by the boys and men but the girls and women could do a pretty good dance.

No one was shy and all that counted was that we were having a good time after a long, hard week working in the fields and woods.

Looking back to those days I often wander how we lived through The Great Depression. We had to grow our food, Make our clothes and find our entertainment wherever we could.

But every neighbor looked for their neighbor. The families were close knitted with each other and shared whatever they had with each other.

Although they were only a few scattered around the old Battery Powered Radio was a very important part of growing up in the mountains of Western North Carolina,

I write these accounts of my early days in the 1930s for

My children, grand children and other young people to remind them that all the things that we have today have not always been here. A vision, hard work and a love for others has brought us to the good life of the year 2008.

# Train Rides

The first train ride that I can remember was when we went to live near my mother's father in Greeley Colorado. Our house in North Carolina burned down, so Grandpa mailed us train tickets for our family to come live near them. This was in the year 1927 and I was only five years old. I am now eighty six but I still remember that old "Coal Burning" engine as it "Huffed and puffed "through the tunnels and over the steep slopes of the Rocky Mountains. Sometimes it had to have helped to keep moving. This was when another coal fired engine would get behind the cars of the "Main Train" and give it a push until it was over the top of the mountain. We didn't move very fast but this didn't make a difference. We were in no hurry, as long as we were moving along everyone was happy. If there was another train on these tracks, and they were going in the opposite direction, one of them would get on a "Side Track", and wait until the other had passed. Then we were on our way on the "main track".

I don't remember how many days it took to make this trip.

We returned to Western North Carolina in 1929. This was during the "Great Depression". This trip back was somewhat different than the train trip. We came back in a "T MODEL FORD". Yes—a "T Model" Ford. I do remember how long this trip was. With dad driving as much as he could stand, both day and night, the trip was eleven days. You must remember in the year 1929 the roads were poor, only a few were paved. Also the towns and villages were few and far apart. This caused some problems also. Plans had to be made to purchase enough food for our meals until we found another place to buy food and gas. By no means was the trip a vacation type thing as we would conceder it to day.

There were no McDonalds or Hardies places to eat. Mom would sometimes cook our meal along side the road. We eat mostly from canned foods.

It was about five years later that I rode "The Train" Again.

We lived in a section of Haywood County that was known as "Mingus Cove". This was nearly two miles from the town of Canton. The railway tracks were near by. They were through a deep cut in a small mountain type hill. The tracks were very steep and when the engine pulling the cars behind it reached the top of this "Cut" in was moving very slow. About the speed of a person walking. Many times when going home from town we would get in an open freight car and ride home. When it was at its slowest speed we would jump from the open door to the side of the tracks. This was a free ride home. Sure better than walking.

These free rides were great but the unexpected had to happen. This was when mom sent my brother, TJ and me to buy a few groceries from the store at the paper mill. This was called "The Company Stores" It was the largest story around and all the employees that worked in the mill could

Buy and they would deduct this from the earnings for working in the mill.

Our grocery list was one 24 lb. sack of self-rising flower, 5 lbs. sugar, box of salt and a glass of "Bruton Snuff".

Mom had us look at the flowery pattern on the last flower sack. Now you be sure and get this same cloth, I'm going to make Louise a new dress. (Louise was our oldest sister).

With the grocery list and our orders for getting the cloth to match what mom already had for making the dress, we were off to town and the store.

We did our usual looking around town, window shopping, looking for someone we knew and probably wanting to make ourselves seen. After a while, we would head for the YMCA and a couple of games of pool before going to the store.

We bought the groceries, I would carry the flower and TJ would carry the small items. The shortest route home was to walk the railroad track. It just happened that a freight train was getting ready to go the route toward our house.

Why we don't ride the train, "I said to TJ." When it gets to the top of the Mingus cut it is hardly moving and very easy to get out of the empty car. We've rode it before. Yeah, said TJ, but we didn't have all these groceries. It was easy to jump out without anything to unload. But it will be better than walking and carrying this heavy load.

We found a car that as empty and the door on the sides was open. We laid the flower and other things in and then climbed aboard our self. We didn't have to wait very long until the train engineer blew some kind of signal with the steam whistle. We were moving and on our way home.

It was not long until the train was laboring real heave to get over the top of the hill and to the level road all the way to Waynesville. Better get out, I told TJ. He didn't have any trouble getting out with his share of our groceries. Next I jumped out with my sack of flower. I wasn't as lucky as TJ. When I jumped it so happened that the sack with the flower was caught on a nail or some sharp object on the side of the door. Here I went, there was a ripping sound and flower was going in all direction with the help of a good wind. I was out and safely on the ground beside TJ.

What we are going to tell momma, TJ said. She sure will be mad not only about loosing the flower but about the cloth for Louise's dress. We will tell her the truth about what happened and take the punishment we deserve.

When we were home and telling mom what happened she was real mad for a short time then she gave us a good lecture and that this was never to happen again. It was not about our riding the train but about lye loss of the flower and the cloth. We both made promises that we would never try to bring anything home on the train. This case was closed; we had learned a lesson from this "Train Ride".

We rode the "Slow Trains" many times later but I had another bad experience on a ride to Waynesville. It was when my uncle "Clifford", my mom's youngest brother and I were going to Waynesville to enlist in the CCC camps. I was 17 and he was 19.

We found us an empty rail car and made our self comfortable. This was what we called a "Local". A train with only one engine that would stop in Waynesville to germ more water for the steam boiler on the ending. This would be the time we would get off.

As we were going through the Mingus cut we noticed that the train was moving faster than it usually did. We had not noticed that another engine had coupled to the first one. There were two engines pulling us along. This was what we called a "Double Header". This train would not stop in Waynesville. It would keep going toward Murphy.

"How are we going to get off?" I asked Clifford.

"We will jump out the door when we get to Waynesville."

"We may get hurt," I said.

"Nah, it will be going slower through town and we will jump."

Soon we were going through "Frog Level". The engineer was blowing the whistle and had slowed down. Clifford jumped out and landed on his feet. "Come on," he said. I was a little scared, but out I went. I wasn't as lucky as Clifford was. I landed on my knees. Here I went, sliding on the coal cinders beside the tracks. I had worn the best pair of pants that I owned. A pair of white corduroy pants. When I got to my feet and was wiping the cinders off me noticed that the knees were torn. My best pair of pants was ruined.

We rode the trains several more times but we always checked to see how many engines they had.

My next train ride was from Fort Bragg, North Carolina to Fort Dix, New Jersey. This was after I finished basic training and was moving north getting ready for overseas assignment. Nothing unusual happened on this trip other than we were on several "Side Tracks" to let other trains pass us. When we made these stops, some of the soldiers would run to a near-by store and buy beer or something to eat, I stayed put. I didn't want to be left behind when the train got underway again.

My last train ride before going to England was the emergency trip from Fort Dix to Canton. The Red Cross contacted me and said that I needed to go home. My dad was in the hospital. They gave me a train ticket to make the trip telling me that the price of the ticket and that they expected me to pay them for it with my next months pay.

I packed a few clothes and a driver took me to the train station in Trenton. I was soon on my way home.

We made several stops between Trenton and Canton.

Nothing unusual happened until we were at Black Mountain, North Carolina. It seems that we stopped at a lot of stores along the way. Sometimes to leave mail and other times to pick-up other things. There were several tunnels that we went through. The conductor would come through the cars and tell the passengers to shut all the windows. Sometimes someone would leave a window down and when we entered the tunnel the passenger car would fill with black smoke from the smoke stack of the engine. Sometimes it would be so thick that your arms and face would be black.

This was my last train ride until we were in England.

While I was in England I rode the trains a lot. This was the main mode of getting from one place to another. Their train cars were different from the ones in the USA. They had private-like compartments where our cars were one room. I kind of liked this privacy, especially if you were riding with a pretty English girl.

I often think what a thrill it would be for the young people today to take a "Real Train Ride" like the ones that we did in the 1930s and 1940s.

Was this what we now refer to as "The good old days"?

# Hog Killing Time

One of the most exciting days of late fall or early winter, usually on Thanksgiving or shortly after , the big day that everyone looked forward to every year was called "hog killing time." This would mean that there would be a big feast of fresh cooked meat on the dining table for several days following the hog killing.

You never killed your hogs on a warm day. The weather had to be near the freezing point to consider it the perfect time. As with all other customs and the way that everything had to be done by the people in the mountains of western North Carolina, killing of hogs was a ritual. The hogs had been feeding and getting their winter's supply of nutrition for a full year, and the people were not going to chance the possibility of loosing any of this meat. This would be their supply of meat until the next hog killing.

There were a lot of preparations before the day that the killing took place. The location had to be near a good supply of water. For my family, this was always near the creek where my brother and I took our weekly bath. There was the hanging pole to make. This was for hoisting the hog up to a vertical position with his head hanging down. Next there was the fire place with the dipping vat. This was made from a large metal drum cut in half lengthwise. The fireplace was made from field stone stacked together to hold the dipping vat. It was usually a couple of feet off the ground to allow for the wood that was used for the fire. A table was made from any lumber that was available. It was used for laying the hog on for removing its hair.

We would get up very early on the day of hog killing. There was a still lot of work to do before killing the hog. We built a roaring fire under the dipping vat in which water was placed the day before. With the fire going real good, we would head back to the house for some breakfast. It would be a long day, and we didn't know when we would be in a position to stop long enough to eat again. This was a job that you could not stop and start when you wanted to. Every step of the ritual had you moving according to plans.

Then we would we go to the hog pen with a hammer, a 22 caliber gun, and a long, sharp butcher's knife. Dad would remove some of the boards from the back of the hog pen, shoot the hog between the eyes, pull him out of the pen, and cut his throat with the butchers knife. This seemed gruesome, but the hog had to be bled this way for the meat to be of first quality for our table this winter.

Next the hog was loaded on a one horse sled and taken to the dressing area. After scalding the hog in the boiling water and removing its hair, a one horse singletree was used to prepare for hoisting to a vertical position and the beginning of butchering.

The one doing the cutting had to be very careful not to cut the intestines. The intestines were caught in a large wash tub and sent to the house where the women could remove the fat for rendering for the grease to make lard shorting and lye soap. When everything was removed from the inside of the carcass and it was washed real clean with water that my brother and I carried from the creek, the body was laid on the table that had also been cleaned. Next was the removal of the ribs, back-bones, and tenderloin. The rough blocking (cutting) was done, and the pieces were sent to the house where they would be placed for cooling until the next day.

Now the work for the men was nearly through for the day. They only had the cleaning up of the cleaning area and putting everything back to its storage place. The big part of hog killing was about to begin with the women doing the bigger part of saving the meat. In addition to rendering the lard, there was sausage to make and can, livermush to make from the liver, canning the tenderloin, ribs, and backbones. They would be in the kitchen where it was very warm from the heat of the wood cook stove.

The children also had to quit their playing and help with grinding the sausage with the hand turned grinder that was fastened to the kitchen table. They didn't want to leave the ball game they were having with the hog bladder. They had washed the bladder real clean, inserted a hollow piece of grape vine and filled it with air by blowing through the hollow of the vine wood and tying it with a string to keep the air in. This was a football, a basketball, and a dodge ball until it became dry and shrank.

The work in the kitchen would go on for about three days. The following morning the final trimming of the hams shoulders and middles was done, and then they were placed on a table that was covered with salt in the smokehouse. When all the pieces were in place they were completely covered with salt. The first stage of curing was complete. Later they would be removed from the salt, cleaned, and rubbed with brown sugar and black pepper. Next they were put in cloth sacks and hung from a pole that was the length of the smokehouse and six foot from the floor. In a few weeks they would be ready for eating.

Back to the kitchen. The sausage, livermush, and cracklings were ready for eating. The best eating was the fried tenderloin along with crackling bread and a glass of cold milk. The livermush and sausage would be eaten later.

Soon all the work that goes with hog killing was finished. We all were filled with good fresh meat from the hog and were ready to get back to our normal routines. This was setting by a fire in the fireplace, popping corn in the wire corn popper and listening to a story told by one of the grown folks. Hog killing was over until about this time next year.

## Saturday Night Bath

When I was growing up in the mountains of Western North Carolina, there was one event that came every week. This was fifty-two times a year and always on a Saturday. And usually the time would be just before we were going to bed for the night. What we did was take our "Saturday night bath." Although we did bathe every day with what we called "wash down as far as possible and up as far as possible", but the whole bath was every Saturday night.

This was not as simple as you may think. There was quite a bit of planning and lots of work in this weekly ritual, and it involved the whole family, that is except for Dad. He usually did his bathing at the paper mill where he worked There were modern bathrooms at the mill complete with a shower room. He took his own soap and towel.

First a large galvanized wash tub was brought into the kitchen. The next thing needed was the water. Here again it took some manual labor to fill the tub with water for the bath. This usually was the job for TJ, my younger brother, and me. Some places that we lived at had a spring. This meant that there were many trips from the house to the spring with our ten quart water buckets. In our younger days this was quite a task because we were not strong enough to carry a full bucket of water and had to make a lot of trips to the spring.

At other places we lived we usually had a hand dug well with a well box and a windlass with a rope and a water bucket. The bucket was tied to one end of a rope which was wound around the wooden windlass. We would unwind the rope until the water bucket was sunk below the top of the water in the well. Next we would crank the windlass until the bucket with the water was near the top where we could grab-hold and empty it into the tub. We would only fill the tub about half way full. We would fill several large cooking pots and set them on our old wood burning stove. When this water began to boil we poured it in the tub of cold water until it was warm enough to bathe in.

The order of bathing was that the oldest person was always first. The bathing then continued down the line according to age until the youngest was given a bath. Sometimes the water was a bit dirty for the last bather. It depended on how many children there were in the family.

We always used soap for bathing, but sometimes we didn't have "store bought" soap. We then had to use the soap that Mom had made from the excess fat from the hogs that were slaughtered at hog killing. This was a very strong soap that was made from the grease of the fat with lye added. Sometimes the lye had to be made from burning wood and collecting the lye from the ashes. If you were not very careful the soap would make blisters on the skin.

My brother and I sometimes did our bathing in the creek that was close to our home. In the warm summer months this was fine. Not only did we stay clean, but there were some places where the water was deep enough for us to swim. In the cold months of winter we would sometime be brave enough to get in the creek.

A sad note about the creek that we bathed in many years ago: It is now only a trickle of water running down through the fields. I was visiting the community where we lived in the 1930s and saw the sad condition of our favorite bathing place. Only enough water is flowing call it a branch instead of a creek. This is was the year 2007.

My oldest son, Gary, asked me how an adult could bathe in such a small place as the wash tub. I explained that first you would sit in the tub with your legs hanging on the outside. You washed the part of your body that was in the tub then stood up in the tub and finished washing your legs and feet.

This was no problem for us children. We could sit in the tub with our feet inside. We were mountain people and were taught by our elders the way to survive and do the many things that had to be done without any outside help. After all, we didn't have the many things that we have today to make life a lot easier with our daily tasks.

We did survive, we kept our body clean, and we had our "Saturday night bath" in the 1930s.

# Wash Day, 1930s

If the words, "wash day" were mentioned today, in 2008, very few people would know what you were talking about. Only the "old-timers" like me and a few of the younger generation who heard about it from their grandfathers or some other person who grew up back in the 1920s and 1930s would know.

Wash day was usually on the same day every week. This was usually on a Monday and lasted through Tuesday, and for a very large family it would be sometime Wednesday before it was completed.

Wash day as we know it today means turning some dials, pushing a button, and adding some washing detergent. There is no certain day for this now. Only when the modern, automatic washer is loaded with dirty clothes do we do the laundry. There are no outside clothes lines for drying the washing. We just move the clothes from the washer to the dryer and push another button. We sit down, read a book, or watch TV until the buzzer sounds telling us the drying is completed. Very few of the things that we wash ever are ironed. Most everything is "wash & wear". This means that there are no wrinkles and the crease is the same as before washing. Even with all these conveniences, we often hear, "I dread tomorrow. It's wash day."

Let me tell you what took place on wash day when I was growing up in the 1930s and early 40s. The day for wash day was always decided by the woman of the home. This was the way it should be because she did most of the work and sometimes all of it. The woman of the house would have the older boys cut the fire wood and fill the boiling pot and the rinsing tubs with water. This was done the night before or early on wash day before leaving for school.

I'm thinking that Monday was chosen for wash day because the only relaxation and rest the women got was on Sunday afternoon after the Sunday dinner was finished. Usually there was no cooking on Sunday night. We had to eat whatever was left over from the noon meal if there was anything. There was usually an extra cake of corn bread that we could eat with a cool glass of milk from the spring box. The spring box was where the milk, butter, or any other food that needed to be kept cool was stored. As with the washing machines today, there were no refrigerators then. Even if there had been any of these conveniences, we couldn't have used them. There was no electric power in the communities around the mountains of Western North Carolina. Only the city folks had electric lights. The electrical gadgets, as we called them, were not invented at this time of the 20th Century. Later in the 30s there were hand cranked clothes wringers for us country people and the ones for those who had electricity were turned by an electric motor.

Now, back to wash day at our house. The wood was cut for the fire to boil the clothes in the big cast iron pot. All the rinse tubs (three) and the boiling pot were filled with water from the spring or the hand dug well. The source depended on where we were living. At one place we lived the well was close to one hundred feet deep. We would lower a bucket tied to a rope and bring up the water. It took some time to fill the pot and tubs.

I or my brother TJ would start the fire around and under the big iron boiling pot. After this we went off to school. Mom was on her own. As soon as it was light enough, here came Mom with the first load of clothes to be washed. She had sorted the white things from the colored. Whites were always the first to be washed. She had a washing stick about five feet long. This was for placing the clothes in the boiling water, stirring them while boiling, and moving them to the first rinsing tub.

The pot was loaded and next to be added was a bar of home-made soap. This was made at hog killing time. It consisted of the excess fat from the hog mixed with caustic lye made from the ashes of wood. This strong soap along with the boiling removed any dirt or stains from the things being washed.

Mom didn't have a watch to time the boiling, but she knew the correct boiling time and would remove them with the washing stick. This stick helped mom do two things with her washing. First, she didn't have to get too close to the fire and risk getting her clothes on fire. The other purpose was to remove the hot clothes from the pot to the rinse tubs.

After all the things to be washed had gone through the pot to tubs they were wringed by hand to remove all the water that was possible. They were then hung on a clothes line or a wire fence if there was one near by. This was their home until dry. On the bad days of the winter months they had to be hung anywhere that could be found in the house. But the actual washing always took place outside. Some of the homes had an outside shed or building that was called the wash house. To my knowledge, we were never fortunate to have a wash house. We always did our laundry outside.

When all the washing was hanging to dry, the water from the iron boiling pot was carried into the house. Mom had a scrubbing brush. She was down on her knees scrubbing the wooden floors with that strong soapy water from the washing. When she finished the floors were bleached white. Nothing was wasted around our house. That soap did two things. It washed the clothes and the floors in the house.

After the washing was dry, Mom's work wasn't over. She had the ironing to do. This could wait until the next day. Ironing was much more work and a very hot job, especially in the summer time. Mom had four solid flat-irons that would sit on the cook stove in the kitchen or on the hearth in front of the fire in the fire place. She would put her forefinger on her tongue to dampen it. After wrapping a cloth around the handle of the iron to keep from getting burned, she would touch the bottom of the iron to check how hot it was. She knew if it was ready by the sound, (hiss) it made when the damp finger touched the bottom. Although the women in this mountain area did not have lot of education, they had a lot of common sense knowledge and ways of doing the things that had to be done. They knew how to make the starch for ironing by mixing wheat flower with water and how thick to make it.

This ritual went on fifty-two times every year and sometimes more than fifty-two. I never heard my Mom complain about her work. She would sometimes say that she was a little tired. But never too tired that she wouldn't cook three meals every day except Sunday. This was the evening we would "snack."

In the late 30s and early 40s there was a washing machine with a roller wringer being sold by Sears and other large companies. The power for operating this machine was a small gasoline engine similar to the ones on the lawn mowers today. It made a lot of noise. This, along with the fumes from the gasoline engine, meant that this modern machine had to be outside when running. Very few people had one of these. Most people didn't have the money to buy one.

I record these accounts of how we lived before all of our push-button things came along. Maybe the generation of today will read this and realize how their forefathers and foremothers did the chores that had to be done.

# Haints, Ghosts, And Boogers

The people that lived in the mountains of Western North Carolina believed in many strange things. They planted different things in their gardens according to the signs of Zodiac and position of the moon. They also believed in the supernatural. They were believers in "Haints, Ghosts and Buggers". If one of the children did something that they were not supposed to they were threatened by their parents. "The haints, ghosts or buggers will get you". This usually did the job. The children believed there were such things.

There is a difference in these three "Supernatural" threats.

The one used depended on how bad a thing you did.

The "Bugger" was used for the lesser punishment. These were the things that were under your bed and would do you harm after you went to sleep. One of these threats would have us keeping our head under the covers on the bed.

Next was the "Ghosts". This was where you would see white sheets and other scary objects floating around in the dark. It was thought that they would get you under their sheet and carry you away.

The "Haint" (haunt) was the really bad one. It was meaner than the others. These were where you would see someone riding a white horse with his head in his hand. You could actually see the blood on the white sheet he would be wearing. Other times there would be some sort of thing flying over your head dressed in white and screaming and making other scary noises. This was the one we were most scared of.

The story begins when we were living in the Piedmont section of North Carolina. My dad quit working in the paper mill and we moved to Gastonia. My grandma, dad's mother,

Had a large house where she kept boarders. They were workers in one of the many cotton mills that didn't' have a home. Cotton was the king of this area and the mills were hiring anyone that applied for a job. This along wit his mother living here was a factor in our relocating to this area.

We had lived here about one year when mom began to think that she wanted to visit her family back in Western North Carolina. Dad agreed that my mom, sister, brother and I could go on the train for a visit. He would get the tickets and schedule. Mom was to write a letter to grandpa Pressley telling him when we would be there.

Mom began to prepare for the train ride. We didn't have any luggage for taking our clothes. Mom was telling grandma about this problem.

"I think I can help you," she said. "I'll borrow a suitcase from one of the boarders." She did get one and mom wasted no time getting what clothes we would need for the trip.

We children were really excited about the train ride and that we were going to grandpa Pressley's house.

The big day arrived and we headed for the train station that was located on the other side of town. This was about a two mile walk for mom who had to carry the suit case and keep us three kids together. We were at the station about one hour before the coal fired steam engine with the passenger cars arrived. Mom didn't want to miss the train. It only went to Canton about once each week.

"All aboard" the conductor hollered. We were in our seats in nothing flat. I got the window seat because I was the oldest. I promised to let TJ and Louise have the window seat on part of the trip. We would be on the train for most of the day. I don't recall what route it took but I know that the train went through the tunnels of Black Mountain before we arrived at the Asheville station. There were many stops along the way. It seemed that we stopped at every village to pick up and leave mail and other things.

Finally in the late evening we arrived at the station in Canton. Grandpa and one of my Uncles were there to meet us. They like most everyone else in the 1930s didn't have a car. We would walk the two or more miles to his house. We didn't mind. We were use to walking every where we went.

Grandpa and grandma and the children that were still living at home lived near the Pigeon River. This is where they built their house when they came back from out west.

After a couple of days we asked where Uncle Fred lived. Grandpa said that it was about a mile to his house. He lived in the section called West Canton. I want to go visit him before we go back home, "I said".

That evening after supper Uncle Clifford, mom's youngest brother who was two years older than me said he would go with TJ and me to visit Uncle Fred.

"Don't stay too late," Mom said. "Something might get you," she joked.

"We are not afraid after dark," I said.

We were soon on our way. When we arrived at Uncle Fred's house, he was setting on the porch talking with one of his neighbors who was visiting. They were discussing nothing in particular, just talking about what had happened since they talked the last time they were together.

The three of us—Clifford, TJ and me—found us a place to set and was listing to everything that they were saying. Uncle Fred must have noticed that we believed what ever they were talking about. He changed the subject.

"Did you hear about the hyena that is prowling around here lately? They say he has killed and eaten several dogs, cats and even a half grown steer. It's not safe to be out after dark, they say."

"Pretty mean critter," his neighbor said. "Shore don't want anything to do with him."

"Another thing that bothers me lately is at that bib pine tree that stands alone beside the road going over to the Pressley house." Fred said.

"Never heard about that, what's taking place at that tree," he said.

"Well, the other day Bill Hall who lives down the road from the Pressleys said he came by there the other night a little after dark and he heard something that sounded like a horse running. He looked up and down the road and didn't see anything. He happened to look toward that big pine and low and behold, guess what he saw."

"What—what—," said Fred's neighbor.

"He swears that there was this big white horse with a rider dressed in white that had no head. At least no head on his shoulders, he was holding his head in his hands and you could see blood running down the sleeves of that white outfit he was wearing. He said that as soon as he saw that horse and the man with his head cut off he headed home as fast as he could run. Said he would never get caught out after dark anywhere near that tree."

Fred's friend began, "there is also talk of a big black panther that someone saw a few nights rite here in West Canton. Been killing some cattle, I hear. And how about that snake that is nearly ten feet long. Been swallowing half grown pigs, not even bothering to chew them. They say that snake could eat a ten or twelve boy.

By this time they had done what they wanted to do—scare the 'day-light' out of Clifford, TJ and me. I knew the tree they were talking about. You could see it from Grandpa's house. Grandma had pointed it out to me the day before.

"See that big pine up there beside the road," she said. "Old Jack, my pet crow has a nest up in the top of that tree. He carries everything he sees around the house that is shiny up to that tree I'm going to get one of the boys to climb up there one day and get all the things he has stolen."

It had become real dark; Clifford had gone inside and gone to bed. He wasn't going back this night. He had been convinced that either the hyena or that headless man would get him. TJ was thinking the same.

"We better get back to grandpas," I said.

"I'm not going out in this dark," he said. "You can go if you like; I'm going inside and get in bed with Clifford. I'm spending the night with Uncle Fred."

I'll show them that I'm not afraid of that Hyena or that man on the horse. I'm going back to grandpa's house. Off I went.

I was walking at my regular pace, but began to think I was hearing noises along the side of the road. I came in sight of the pine tree and began to walk a little faster. Soon I was running as fast as I could. I didn't slow down until I was in the yard at the house.

Everyone was still up. No one had gone to bed. They were waiting for us to come back from Fred's.

"Where are Clifford and TJ?" someone asked.

"They decided to spend the night with Uncle Fred," I said. I didn't' dare tell them about the haints, nor did I tell them that I had run the last mile on my way back. I think they knew because I was wet from sweating.

The next morning Clifford and TJ came home. They never mentioned that they were afraid to come home last night.

For the rest of our visit with Grandpa, TJ and I never ventured out after dark. We didn't want to take any chances of meeting any "Haints" that roamed the mountains of Western North Carolina. We would take our chances with ghosts and boogers, but not the haints. They were the meanest.

# Friends

Have you ever thought about where the friends that you had many years ago are now? Where they live, what they are doing and the many questions we ask ourselves.

Let's close our eyes... forget all the things that are happening around you, drift back as far as you can remember and ask yourself, who was my friend back in such and such time? I wonder where are they now? Wonder if they ever married and had children? There is no end to the many questions we have about the past and the many friends of our life.

Let's start back when we were near eight years old. Our close friends were Lester, Bill, Bob and on and on. These were the neighbor's boys and my friends. They were the ones than would visit and we were off to the woods. Climbing the skinny saplings and playing Tarzan. We made it real, every thing but the monkeys, lions and snakes. The stumps and fallen trees were our wild animals. We had a good imagination,

Only a few years when passed when Lester, Bill and Bob were replaced with Fanny, Betty, Edith and many more.

These were our new friends. They didn't like the games of Tarzan, Tex Ritter and the heroes of the movies. They preferred Shirley Temple, Little Orphaned Annie, play house and the many things young girls liked. They were not about to change to think like us boys did. We had to change to what they wanted to do. At least when we were with them.

Then came the High School years and not only had we forgot about all the games us boys played but the girls were also changing. Although we all had fun as a group at dances, parties corn shucking and other grouped gatherings there were times we preferred to be alone. One boy, one girl. This was the serious time for talking, a little petting and a good visit with each other.

Then WW II came along and this was the parting of the long time friends. We were to be with many different people from other countries that talked differently from the way we talked in them mountains of western North Carolina. Not only did the talk differently, they, had a different outlook of life and the food that they eat was different. I liked some of the changes that the had especially the different types of food.

I was soon eating food that I had never seen or heard of.

I also made new friends that were from different parts of the USA.

There was Rooster, the German, the Indian chief, the country singer, and others that were nicknamed for something noticeable about them. They gave me the name of Slim. I wonder why? I weighed 130 pounds, stood 6 ft., 1 in. tall and was 20 years old.

Rooster must have come from the farm somewhere because he was always imitating chickens. His favorite was crowing like a rooster. The German was a fellow from Saint Louis Missouri. His name was Panhorst. We hit it off from the start.

The other new friend was the Indian. His name was Brezeale.

He was from the Cumberland Mountains of Tennessee. Then Later on after basic training I met Bill Grooms. He was our supply sergeant. He was a Dutchman from somewhere up north. These were my closes friends all through the war.

Of course I made many friends with the people of the countries that I was in. Most of the ones I remember were the many pretty girls of England, France Belgium and Germany.

I soon forgot all of their names except two of the girls in England. For some reason their name wouldn't go away like all the others. One was the daughter of the manager of the laundry where we took our company laundry every week. The other was a 17 year old girl that worked at this laundry.

After 28 months away from the US, I had survived the war and was getting ready to go home. I was ready and looking forward to the many little things that I missed, Things like a glass of cold milk, a hot dog with all the trimmings—especially lots of chili without the beans that our northern friends add to their chili. And, of course, my family and long-time friends.

I didn't expect to find that some of them never came back from the war, others that didn't go to war had married and moved away to some other city where they were working during the war. It seemed that every body and every thing was not the same as when I left. There were no Saturday night square dances or parties that we attended before.

Everyone had gone their separate way. I had to adjust to this new way of life.

I married a girl that I had known for many years. I went off to school in Chicago with my new bride. She worked to pay the rent and buy the food while I attended school. Soon I graduated and we returned to North Carolina. I went to work for the paper mill in their electric department. We soon had a new son, Gary, and a new house. I didn't have time to think about the long time friends of the many years past. I was busy helping to raise a family. Soon there was another boy in the family, Dean. This also mad a few minor changes in our life style. But for the better. I was working; we had two fine boys, a new house and anew 1951 car. I began to think about some of my army friends. I contacted the German in St. Louis. He invited us to visit him. Plans were made and off we went. We spent a week with him and headed back to North Carolina. The following summer Harley and his wife, Mamie came to North Carolina to visit us.

In 2004, after my wife of 60 years died, I began to search for the war time friends. The first one that I found was the 17 year old (1944) girl that worked at the laundry. I posted an email in one of the local papers in Birmingham, England. About two weeks later I received an email from her grandson saying that she was well and that she would like to talk with me. I emailed him and set a date to make the call. I did call and since then we have exchanged mail and calls to each other. I had found a long time ago friend. Over 60 years had gone by. She had raised a family and so had I.

The next old time friend that I was to locate was the "Country Singer," James Foster. I located him in a small town in North Carolina called Cooleemee. The population is near 6,000. I have called and talked with him several times. He is married, they had one Daughter that was killed in an accident when only 17 years old. Although I invited him to visit me he declined. The reason being the same as mine. To old to travel a long distance.

The next army buddy I was able to locate was "The Chief"—his name is Clearance Breazeal. I located him in Morristown, Tennessee. He is married also, but never had any children. He to declined to visit me. His wife is very ill, and he has to stay close-by.

I will continue looking for my childhood friends and the friends that were in the army with me. They are like me—getting old and content to be close to home. I will be 86 on my next birthday, April 1, 2008.

If I do not find any others, I have been blessed to have so many good friends during the 85 years of my life. I am thankful for a long and good life that I have had. God has been good to me.

# Labor Day, 1930s

I remember in the early days of my childhood how we celebrated the holidays. There were not as many as there are today. We had Christmas, Easter, Thanksgiving, 4th of July, New Year's Eve and Labor Day.

Christmas was my favorite, and the next holiday that I looked forward to was "Labor Day". Why Labor Day?

Labor Day was when the carnival (or midway) came to Canton with all the rides, cotton candy and several small tents with games of skill. There were also the "Flim-Flam" tents. This was where you made a bet then guessed which shell had the pea under it. The person operating this game was very quick with his hand movements. Regardless of which shell you picked the pea wouldn't be there. He had it in his hand and when he lifted the shell with the pea he actually drooped it from his hand. This was a "No-Win" game.

Months before Labor Day we would start planning and saving our pennies and nickels. Money was scarce and we would be lucky to have as much as $2.00 by the time the rides came to town. My brother and I would cut firewood for our neighbors. Sometimes we would plow or work in the hay field. We were usually paid ten cents an hour. We would also sell eggs to the stores if we happened to have extra ones. The store keeper would pay a penny each. We would do any odd job for a few nickels and dimes in order to have "Labor Day" money.

The "Lee Rides" were always here exactly one week before Labor Day. This was true seventy years ago and they are still coming on the same schedule today. They could set up their rides anywhere there was room for them. They brought their gas motors to turn the electric generator to make electricity for the lights and motors that were on the rides. They had to be ready for any location because most vacant fields that they had to use didn't have any electric power. There were very few homes with electricity outside of the towns that they took the rides to. This was true in Canton North Carolina during the 30s and 40s. There were very few homes with electric power until after WW II.

Starting in the late 40s the TVA and the Government started a program called "Rural Electrical Association".

This plan supplied electric power to all rural sections of our area and I suppose other areas as well.

Carried away from our story a little bit but thinking this would explain why the rides were self supplied with their needs.

On Labor Day morning everyone at our house was up a little earlier than usual. After all, this day, like Christmas, was for one day only and we didn't want to miss a single thing that took place that day at the "Rides and shows".

There was breakfast to be cooked for mom. My brother, TJ

Had milking to do and I would feed the hogs and chickens. It was so early that the chickens were still on their roost but they would find the food when it became light later on in the morning. Everyone knew what needed to be done before leaving for town. We had been through this annual ritual many times before.

TJ, my brother and I were the first leave, heading toward town. A little later mom and the two girls, my sisters, Louise and Leveta. They were younger than me and TJ and they were girls, they had to have more," Looking After" than we boys.

When we arrived I would guess that it was near eight AM. The rides were running but no one was on them. They were checking to see if everything was working properly and was safe to ride on.

It wasn't long until there was a pretty good crowd. Mostly men and young boys. The women and little children would always be the last ones to get here.

Those rides and tents where there were games of chance were open and a few were on the rides. No one was in any hurry because it would be a long day. No one went home until everything was closed. This was usually around eleven thirty

It was nearing noon and you would see a bunch of men gathered off to themselves. They were chewing their tobacco, smoking a pipe, telling tall tales and swapping pocket knives. Families that brought a picnic lunch were opening their baskets getting ready to eat dinner.

There was one senior that had his dinner time solved. Uncle Billy would buy a small watermelon from the truck

That brought a load every Labor Day. He always sold all that he had because we couldn't grow tem in Western North Carolina. The summer sunshine was not around long enough for a melon to ripen. Uncle Billy would find him a place away from the crowd, bust that melon open by hitting it on his knee. He didn't have a fork or spoon. He eat that

Watermelon with his fingers. He didn't care if someone was watching, he kept right on eating with the juice running through his beard that he had.

Everyone was at the rides by now. Some eat at home before coming. Boys ad girls began to pair up. Not a boy and a girl, but a boy with his best friend and the girl with her friend. The girls that wouldn't even give you a second look at school would make it a point to get real close to the boys' the would do their little "Giggle". Bat their eyes at you and give you one of the biggest smiles you ever had. Now,

All of this attention meant only one thing. They were trying to get a free ride on the ferries wheel or swings, Some of the boys fell for this "Lovey-Dovey" stuff and spent as much as fifty cents on them. But you just wait until the next day at school. The giggle the smile and the rolling of their eyes were gone. Everything was back to normal for the Boy-Girl thing until next Labor Day

Everyone men, women, boys and girls would wander from ride to ride, booth to booth all day long just watching those that had money to spend try to knock the milk bottles down, and win a "Guppy Doll" for someone special. This was true at the rides. Just stand there watching to see if someone got scared and did a lot of screaming or what ever. This was a day for visiting; forget all the hard work that had to be done before winter set in and the cold snow days ahead.

This Labor Day celebration was every year that I can remember while growing up. It is still being held the same as seventy years ago The same ride companies, "Lee Rides" The changes are that there are more rides, the people attending have more money to spend, including the young girls. They don't have to play the game the used in the 30s to get rides. They spend on the boys to get them to ride with them. Sure wish it was like this in the "Good Old Days".

I do not know if the crowds and the excitement are still there. It would be nice if I would go back some Labor day and see all the changes. Who knows? I just might run into one of the smiling girls from the 30s. I don't think they would recognize me or would I them. Maybe someone would introduce us to each other? I don't think she would care to ride the swings or ferries wheel, not even the ponies on the merry go round. I know for sure that I would decline an invite. At 86 years old my biggest thrill is rocking real high in my favorite rocker or swinging in the swing under the maple tree.

This is only one of the many "Fun Days" we had when I was a kid. There were others but besides Christmas, "Labor Day" was my favorite day of the year

# Saturday, 1930s

Living in the mountains of Western North Carolina following the great depression was not an easy life by no means. Everyone made life a little easier by having dreams of a better day and looking forward to some special event that may come their way.

As a young boy growing up under these conditions my dream, along with my brother and other friends was the week end when Saturday rolled around. What made this day different from any other days of the week? We always managed to have enough money for the movie and sometimes a hotdog. If we were to sacrifice one or the other it would be the hotdog. We were hooked on the Saturday movies,

There was several ways for us to earn the ten cents for the movie and the dime for the hotdog along with a Ne-Hi Soda. I had a couple of chickens that I could save the eggs and sell at one of the two local general stores. They would give me a penny for each egg. This was that each hen had to supply me with five eggs every week for the movie money. The other money came from helping the neighbors cut wood or other work on their farm. One of our neighbors was handicapped and the only work that he could do was shine shoes at the barbershop in town. He walked beside the railroad track on his way home every evening. He would bring one of the discarded rail ties home for fire wood. He couldn't cut it for the stove. My brother and ma cut the ties for his stove wood. We would cut the wood early on a Saturday morning. Wash and change clothes, go to the barber shop and he would give each of us a quarter. That quarter bought the hotdog, a Ne-Hi drink and left a dime for the movie.

Sometimes I would find empty wine bottles on the side of the road that I would sell for a nickel each to one of the local "Bootleggers". They usually were one half pint size and sometimes called "Bat wing". A "Bootlegger" was someone that sold moon shine, (Home Made Whiskey).

They bought the whiskey in half gallon glass jars and reduce them to several smaller sizes to sell. The smaller size would sell for fifty cents, (Half Pint) and the half gallon for five dollars. He sold more of the smaller sizes because his customers were poor and didn't have a lot of money.

One day my brother, TJ, his friend and I were walking home from school. We were taking a short cut through the woods and happened to pass a saw dust pile where there had been a saw mill. TJ kicked a pile of sawdust and out came a half gallon jar of moonshine. Some bootlegger had hid it here. We took a good look around to see if anyone was watching us. I picked up the jar and we headed for our house. TJ's friend and I divided the half gallon and he took a quart and left me the same. I sold my half for fifty cents but TJ didn't get any money from our find and he was the one that found it,

When Saturday came I was off for town as soon as I finished my chores around home. I walked everywhere I went and 4 or 5 miles didn't bother me at all.

I would get to town at least an hour before the Movie house opened, (10 am) and circle the three city blocks that made-up the town of Canton. I was looking for one of my buddies to go to the movies with me. It was always more fun to have someone to help you pull for the "Good Guys" in the western. They wouldn't have survived all the shooting from the "Bad Guys" without us yelling and telling them where they were hiding. If they were to get shot there wouldn't be a show next Saturday. We were into the show so deep that we really believed this to be so. After all, we were 10- and 11-year-old country boys.

At 10 o'clock the movie house would open and start selling tickets, At 10:30 the show would begin. At first there would be some advertising. Then the previews for the next week show. Then the excitement began. There would be a cartoon of Mickey Mouse or Popeye. We loved Popeye and his strength after eating his spinach. He got lots of us boys to eating swinish even when we didn't like it.

Next there would be a serial show. This would be a Tarzan or some similar movie that would be shown for about 15 minutes and then continued until next Saturday. It would stop at some point where the star was in great danger and kept us trying to figure out how he would save himself.

Then the great moment arrived, "The main feature".

It would be Hoot Gibson, Hop-along Cassidy. Tim McCoy or the Lone Ranger. Usually the movie would have a western Band singing the most popular western songs. We usually kept our seats until we had seen the movie at least two times and sometimes more than two. We would leave humming the songs from the show or imitating Popeye.

The rest of the day we spent wandering up and down the three city blocks of "Main Street". Looking for some friends and window shopping. There was no going home until the stores closed and everyone heading for home. By the end of the day we had all the latest news and what had happened since the past Saturday.

After I became a teenager I began to think of other forms of entertainment on the Saturdays. Of course the movies never stopped but I would only see it one time. My friends that were my age had noticed or heard of other "Fun" place away from town. These places were known as "Honker Tonks". There were three that catered to the teenagers. These were, the weeping Willow located one the Asheville Highway. The one toward Waynesville on Hwy. 19-23 called Little Rock. The one that we didn't visit very often was Candler Springs. This was too far away from Canton. All of these places had a juke box with the latest music and a dance floor. They sold soft drinks along with sandwiches and snacks. No alcohol drinks were allowed. I went to the Weeping Willow every time I could catch a ride, It was located about two miles from town. I would buy a "Big Orange" soda, find a good seat with some friend and watch the "City Girls and Boys" do the dancing. They were really good dancing the "Jitter Bug" and other modern dances. The only dancing that I knew at this time was the "Old Fashion" square dance. It was good clean fun most of the time. Occasionally someone would get their temper up when someone tried to steal their girl friend. This usually ended up with a little pushing and some unkind words. The owner of this place wouldn't put up with any cussing and fighting. He kept a shot gun behind the counter. I believe he would have used it if the party got to rough.

There was one time that I was at the Weeping Willow when my uncle came by with his girl friend. Clifford owned a car. He delivered the Asheville News Paper and had to have a means of going all over the county. He asked if I would like to go with them to Candler Springs. Of course I did because I had only been there once. It was about ten miles from Canton.

It was raining when we arrived and the place was closed for the night. I guess that there was no one out on this nasty, wet night so he had called it a day and locked up.

Clifford turned around and we were on our way back to the Willow. The car began to slide and before he could get it back on the road we were in the edge of a corn field. He tried to get back on the road but nothing happened except the wheels spinning. You two get out and push and I'll try to get back on the road. We were pushing and he was racing the engine. All at once the car jumped forward and we were back on the narrow gravel road. His girl friend and I had mud all over us. You can wash up when we get back to the Willow," he said". This was my last trip to Candler Springs.

Time went by pretty fast and before long I had quit the Saturday journeys to town. I was slowly becoming a man and my thoughts were a lot different now.

Many years have passed in my life but I still think of the good times that I had on, "SATURDAYS—1930s".

# Huckleberry Picking

Better hurry and get the wood chopped and carried in the house and do the feeding before your Dad gets home, Mom said. He promised to take you two with him to camp out tonight and pick huckleberries tomorrow. If you expect to go, you had better get busy.

We had heard many times of the wild animals and other exciting things that were to be seen at Grave Yard Fields in the high places of Cold Mountain. Also the beauty of Shining Rock. All of these places were at an elevation of 5,000 to 6,000 feet. And this is where the huckleberries were. The huckleberry is a wild blueberry and the best ones are found at elevations between 3,500 and 7,200 ft. elevations. All of these places were in what would become the Pisgah National Forest.

All the work at home was done and my brother, TJ and I were all excited and waiting for Dad to get home from his job in the paper mill. It seemed like a life time but pretty soon here comes the "A-Model Ford "and Dad. The wait was over. We're ready, we yelled. "Let's go".

"Wait a minute," Dad said. "We have to take something to eat and buckets to put the berries in. It will take a few minutes so be patient."

He began to pack some things in a "Toe-Sac," (burlap bag).

In went Vienna sausage, sardines, pork and beans, some bacon, a frying pan, some coffee and a coffee pot along with a box of soda crackers. That should be enough food to last for one day. We will have to carry the eggs in a poke, (paper bag), by their self. Don't want to break them before the pan is hot, (laughing).

All the food and buckets were placed in the back seat of the Ford and we loaded up. TJ and me in the back seat, Dad in the driver's seat. Why can't one of us ride up front, I asked? Got to go by Bill's house and pick him up. He is going with us. Bill was one of Dad's drinking buddies, not one that would go out of his way to pick Huckleberries. Although I was only about 12 years old, I sensed that there was more to this trip than berry picking. Just the same, we were in for a treat because we had never ventured this far from home.

We stopped at Bill's house. He had a sack but there wasn't as much in it as there was in our sack. He got in the car and we were on our way up highway 276 going toward Crusoe at the foot of Cold Mountain.

We passed the general store that sold hardware, clothes, groceries, feed for all types of animals and was also the US Post office. My second cousin (by marriage) worked at this store.

About two miles past the store we turned off on a narrow road on the right, the farther up this road we went the rougher and narrower it became.

We were at the end of the road when all of a sudden here comes about six hound dogs barking as loud as they could. The acted like they would eat us alive if they could get in the car. On the steep hillside was an unpainted weather board house with a long porch the full length of the house. A tall lanky man appeared on the porch, His face was thin and he looked like he hadn't shaved for about a month. He had a floppy wide brim hat on his head with the front nearly covering his eyes. One loud word from him and the dogs quit their barking, put their tales between their hind legs and under the house they went.

"Howdy there," he hollowed. "You fellers lost or something?" he said. "Better get out of that car and set a spell. Them hounds wouldn't bite a piece of bread. Just all noise, don't see many people besides our family."

By this time there was a lady and six or eight children of all ages from about two to maybe sixteen. The woman looked old and wrinkled from bearing all of these children and all the hard work taking care of them and her husband. These families that lived back in the hollows at the foot of Cold Mountain were close to each other and seemed to be a happy bunch. Maybe not too well feed but always happy.

They had never experienced any other way of life..

We got out of the car, Dad and Bill shook hands with the man and said howdy to the woman and children.

"Can't stay long," Dad said. "Going Huckleberry picking back on Shining Rock. Like to go as far as we can before it gets dark. Could get lost after dark and besides we got to find a place to camp and gather some fire wood. I haven't been back here since I was a boy. Probably been twenty or twenty-five years. Things have changed since the loggers cut all the trees down. It's a shame; a lot of the wild animals have left to find trees back where they left the trees. They depend on the nuts and berries for their food. It's a shame."

"You fellers want a little drink before you start the steep climb up that mountain? Give you extra strength, you know? Made this myself, good corn licker, none better on this mountain."

Out comes a half gallon mason fruit jar that was so clear that it looked empty. Dad and Bill were grinning from ear to ear. This was too good to be true. This was the start of their getting ready to pick berries. The man removed the lid, took a couple of big swallows and handed it to Dad. He had a few good swallows and passed it to Bill. Thank you. Dad said.

"Mighty fine licker, best I ever tasted," Bill nodded his approval.

"Better get started," Dad said. "Which trail is the best to take leading to the Shining Rock area?"

"You can leave your car here. We will look after it for you. Take that trail over yonder and go about a mile and you will hit an old logging road. Take a left and this goes to the top of the mountain. You can see the rocks from there cause all the trees are gone. Nothing left but scrub trees and fields of huckleberry bushes. Be sure to stop for a spell on your way back, may be a little corn licker left."

Off we went. Up the narrow trail that was steep and rocky.

We soon found the logging road. The walking was a lot better because there was not a lot of rocks and bushes here.

Soon the sun was going down and dusk darkness was coming on. Better stop here for the night," Dad said. "Here is a good wide and sort of level place to make camp. You boys gather up some wood for the fire. Bill and I will clear off a place for the fire."

Off we went. We didn't have to go far because the loggers only took the big part of there trees. There were plenty of dead dry limbs everywhere. Soon there was a big pile of wood. That should be enough, better cut some spruce or hemlock branches for your bed or you will have to lay on the hard ground tonight.

Dad and Bill had gathered rocks and made a circle with them. This was to be where we had the fire. The rocks would keep the fire from getting in the grass and starting a forest fire. Soon the fire was going and TJ and I asked if we were going to cook.

"Not tonight. You can open some pork and beans and eat some crackers. We will cook a big breakfast."

We didn't have to wonder any longer as to what Bill had in his sack. He untied the sack, reached in and out came a half gallon fruit jar. There was no guessing as to what was in that jar. "White Lightning". This was their way of getting the energy to pick the berries the next day.

TJ and I ate our beans and crackers and went to our tree branch beads. Dad and Bill were to keep the fire going and build up their energy with the moon shine.

TJ and I were soon sound asleep. This was not for long because we were awakened by a growl and the rustling of leaves. Dad and Bill were "Dead-to-the-world". That is, they were sound asleep. Not for long—I woke them up. Dad lit the lantern and placed it on his head. He began to look around. Soon he stopped turning his head and said, "it's a bear", and a big one. "Probably smelled the pork and bean cans that you boys were eating. He won't come any closer because he is afraid of the fire."

Although we moved our bed closer to the fire TJ and I didn't sleep very much for the rest of the night. We were afraid that this bear would drag us off into the woods and eat us. We had heard many scary stories about what the wild animals in these mountains would do to children. A loud holler from Dad, "GIT "and that bear was out of here, down the mountain side he went. Dad and Bill lay back down and were soon snoring. The moon shine from last night was still working on them.

Soon it was daylight and we were up and ready for breakfast. Didn't take very long to cook and eat. "Got to get to picking them berries," said Dad. "Soon be time to head back down the mountain. Mom will have to make jelly or can them today or they will sour before tomorrow."

After finishing eating we scraped up some dirt and covered the fire. Didn't want it to get into the woods and start a fire.

This area had been burned several years earlier and killed many of the trees. Didn't want this to happen again.

We were soon headed to the valley where there was an old abandoned rail road and where there were plenty of berry bushes. The railroad was left when the Sunburst logging company quit cutting the trees in this area. There were the stumps from the spruce and fur trees that measured 4 and 5 feet across. These must have been really big giant trees.

Mother Nature was trying to regroup these trees but it will take many years and they will never be like they were before cutting.

We soon had our buckets full of big juicy huckleberries and were doing some exploring along the rail track.

"Better be careful where you step," Dad said. "There are lots of rattle snakes up here. They won't bother you if you don't bother them. If you see one just move on and it will go away."

Dad and Bill were shooting at some Boomers. They were so fast that they never killed one. A boomer is a small squirrel. Larger than a ground squirrel and smaller than a gray or red squirrel. They are only found at high elevations. In the mountains. I do believe they can see your finger move when you start to pull the trigger on your gun. Before the "BANG" they are in another tree or up to the top of the one they are in. Occasionally they will be off-guard and you can kill one, not very often though.

The berries were picked, the moonshine was gone, we were getting hungry and we had the long trip back down Cold Mountain. Off we went, anxious to get home. We had enough of camping out and berry picking.

We were back at the house where the car was and the big happy family that lived there. I never learned of their name. The man that greeted us on our way up was setting on the porch enjoying a big chew of burley tobacco. "Howdy," he said. Better set a spell and rest before leaving, he said. Got to get home so the old lady can take care of these berries. Dad said. Want a swig of my corn before you leave? This was what Dad and Bill was hoping he would say. The effect of the drinking from the night before was nearly gone and they needed a boost. Sure and we are much obliged to you. A couple of big gulps. Wiping their mouth and we were on our way home.

This has been many years ago but I will never forget," "The huckleberry picking".

# Ramp Tramp

Have you ever heard someone talk about "Ramps"? Do you know what a Ramp is? Or what it's used for or where do you find them?

The people of the mountain sections of the south have known what they were, where to find them and what to do with them. They used them for food, and Medicine. They knew how to cook them and what would make a good side dish. There were many plants in the mountains that were edible but the ramp was their favorites. The ramp can be found from South Carolina to Canada, they appear in the Springtime.

They are very popular in the state of West Virginia and the Canadian province of Quebec. They are also very popular in Tennessee and North Carolina Where annual events are held that are referred to as "Ramp Tramps". They are also found in Europe but are referred to as "Wild leek". They are used in cooking quite often.

While hunting in the mountains of North Carolina, I saw ramps very often but never gave any thought as what they were used for. I had heard some of the "Men Folks" talk about eating them when they were in the mountains for several days. They jokingly said that they smelled so bad that no wild animal would dare get close to you.

The popularity of "The Ramp" began to get attention and there were "Ramp Clubs" being formed in different towns and villages. The clubs began gathering together every spring and having what they called a "Ramp Tramp." They elected comities for this annual "Get -to-, Gather". One group would make a trip to the mountains to "Dig" (Harvest) enough to feed the big crowds that attended on the big day of the tramp.

Another committee would contact Blue Grass bands and country singers to entertain the crowd. The next assignment was the "Main" and most important one. "The Cooks". This was a very demanding job. Every cook had to know how much meat, (Bacon or ham) to cook with the ramps, and how long to cook before cooking the scrambled eggs. All the other "fixings" were prepared at home and brought to the celebration. There would be plenty of cornbread, fresh buttermilk and you could bet your last dollar that some "Good Old Boy" would secretly bring a jug of liquid corn.

Of course this wasn't for everyone. Just his close buddies and maybe a little for the music makers.

The celebration started early with the music and singing. While this was going on the cooks were busy getting ready to feed everyone.

After a good meal of ramps, ham, scrambled eggs, ham. Corn bread and a big glass of butter milk to wash all of this down there would be more music and then the dancing began. For those that didn't dance they would gather in small groups and catch up on the news from their last meeting. Everyone enjoyed these, "Ramp Tramp'

The Sunday school class that my brother, TJ and I belonged to at the Oak Grove Church located in the community of Thickety decided to have a ramp tramp of our own. This was after we returned from WW II in the late 1940s. The women of the class were to do the cooking and the men were to go to the mountain and dig the ramps.

As soon as the Sunday services were over several of us loaded up in a couple of cars and headed for the mountains above

Crusoe located at the foot of Cold Mountain. This was where we were going to digging the ramps for our "Ramp Tramp".

We took a couple of big "Burlap sacks" to put the ramps in. The place that we found the ramp patch was a good one. It didn't take us long to fill the sacks and head bock down the mountain, load up and head back to Thickety. We were about half way back when it started raining. We'll have to cook under the "Thickety Community Shed" about a mile from the Church. TJ said, "A little rain is not stopping us from having our ramp dinner."

When we arrived at the community shed the women were already cooking the meat to get the grease for the ramps.

Some of us were cleaning the ramps and others cutting them into small pieces for cooking. The women soon had everything cooked and on the tables along with the corn bread and butter milk which they had prepared the day before. After the blessing by one of the men we were ready for our "Ramp Meal" and none too soon. We all were hungry as a wolf.

By the time we finished eating and cleaning everything it was time for the evening church service. We washed up a little, combed our hair, loaded up in our cars and headed for church.

We all went to our regular seats where we were in a habit of setting. Heads began to turn. People began taking their handkerchiefs out and wiping their eyes and nose. Some even coughed.

The preacher took his place up front and began clearing his throat. It seems that some one has been to the ramp patch, Smells like onions in here. I believe it is worse than onions, more like garlic.

The preacher was looking directly at Howard, TJ's brother-in-law. "It ain't me preacher," Howard said. "I only eat one helping, but TJ and some of the others eat two or three helpings. It's them preacher, not me," Howard said.

"Now wait just a minute, Mr. Dotson. You eat as much as I did and you know it."

The preacher cleared his throat and said, "let's all stands and sings the first and third verse of page 224 in the hymnal on the bench where you are setting. The piano player started the music, the "song leader" stood, and we all began to sing "The Lilly of the Valley".

There was no more talk of how we smelled.

This has been many years ago that I went to a "Ramp Tramp". This was my first and also the last one for me.

# Biscuits And Gravy

When you go to a fast food eating place for breakfast and order, "Biscuits and Gravy", do you ever think about what you are eating or where the ingredients came from? How much work do you think it took to make the flour for the biscuit and gravy?

If you should get egg and biscuits you would know where the egg came from. Or if it be sausage you would know that the sausage was from a hog.

Let us take a look from the beginning as to where we get the wheat flower to make the biscuits and gravy.

I don't know how far back in history where wheat was used for food. The word "wheat" is mentioned 52 times in the Old Testament of the Bible, so I would guess that it has been around from the beginning of time. It is used for food for mankind and food for animals.

Threshing day every year was a big event for the farmers that had wheat for the threshers that came around in the late summer. The owner of the threshing machine in our area was a farmer by the name of Bud Harris. He and his son Jack would do the moving of the machine from farm to farm. The moving was done with a tractor with iron wheels that were near six feet in diameter with iron spikes on them. The "set-up" and keeping the thresher running was the Harris' job as owners. Most of the work was the responsibility of the farmer where the work was taking place. Bud would hire a couple of employees for measuring the grain as it came out of the thresher. The pay was usually twenty or twenty five cents an hour. The farmer would pay the same if he had to hire someone,

The big wheat growers in our community," Thickety ", were, Bud Harris, Wilson Medford, Tom Sorrels, Johnny Willis and ever once in a while Alden Clark had a few stacks.

Sometimes it would take several days to finish at one farm.

The women of the neighborhood were a big part of "Threshing Day". The women from all the farms that were on the threshing schedule would get together where the workers were at. Their job was to feed all of the ones that were working with the threshing. This was no small task because there were a large number of workers.

All the men of the farms that were having threshing would help their neighbors until everyone had their wheat in the storage places. This was a big challenge for the women folks to keep these hungry men feed.

I was close to fifteen years old the summer I worked with the threshers. I was paid twenty cents an hour and had several different job assignments. I cut binds and feed the wheat into the thresher. I helped measure the wheat as it came out of the machine. It requires two people to do the measuring, If the farmer was paying Bud with a tool we would measure seven parts for the farmer and the eighth part went to bud as pay. Some paid him with money. How much, I don't know. I also was on the straw stack helping with the stacking. This was done around a long pole that was set in a hole in the ground. Usually there were two people on the stack and we had to place it around the "Stack Pole" in a way to keep it from sliding off. We did this with pitch forks. The stack of straw, when finished had to be shaped so the water and snow would not stay on or soak into the straw. If it wasn't smooth with a finish that looked pretty, then the person who did the stacking didn't know how to make a straw stack.

At the end of the work day which was from daylight until dark, all the workers had to find some place to take a bath to get the dust and straw off his body. If some of the workers lived to far from where the work was taking place they would spend the night with the owner of that location.

Usually every one left and returned early the next day.

I have only explained briefly about all the hard work that was required to have the wheat for the flour. But in order to have flour the wheat had to be taken to a flour mill and be ground into the fine soft powder we call flour.

Then the cooks take over for making the biscuits and gravy that we have for breakfast. Their job also requires some skill. They have to know exactly how much of each ingredient to add and how long to cook it.

The biscuit is eaten with many other add-on's, but most of the time, it is accompanied by the old stand-by, gravy. The next time you eat breakfast and have these old standards as the main course, take a moment to think of all the hard work that it took so you could have *"Biscuits and Gravy."*

# A Wife For Life

He had become a young adult and one day he said to himself. It's about time I start looking for a wife. Another couple of years and I'll be too old for the pretty young ones to pay me notice.

This was a young man that lived in one of the many coves of Western North Carolina. These people of the many coves and mountains thought that if you never married and raised a family you were one of two things. Off in your thinking (crazy) or a little on the odd side. With this in mind he began to make plans.

He couldn't make up his mind as to a starting point. "I know what I'll do," he said. "I'll write all of the different coves on a separate piece of paper and put them in a box. The name I pull out is where I will start."

He began to write, Buckeye Cove, Dutch cove, Henson Cove, Sorrels Cove, Stamey Cove and a half dozen more.

All the names were put in a shoe box. He put the top on the box and shook it up to mix the names. Off came the lid; in went his hand, out comes the name, Stamey Cove.

"Ain't any girls in Stamey Cove," he said. "I'll go take a look and draw another name."

Off he went, up the Pigeon River and to Stamey Cove.

He was tired and thirsty from the long walk so he stopped a small country store to buy a "Big Orange" soda. When he walked into the store his eyes came out on stymies. There stood two of the pretest girls that he had ever seen. And another thing, they both looked alike. "I've hit the jackpot," he thought to himself.

He had forgotten about the drink. He walked slowly up to the girls and said, "My name is Ben, I live past town in the Buckeye Cove."

They gave him their names and another thing he noticed was that one of them talked a lot and the other was sort of quiet, I think I like the one that likes to talk. If I were to marry her there never would be a dull moment around the house. Yes sir, that's the one. I believe she would make a good wife and mother for my children.

Got to have some kids around to do the milking and plowing. Ben was already dreaming of setting on the front porch when he retired and watching others do all the work that needed to be done around the home.

He wasted no time getting acquainted with his new found love.

"What's your name?" he asked.

"Ruth," she said. "And this is my twin sister. We live up the road a piece. About a half mile, then turn right. You can't miss our house. Our dad raises fighting chickens and you can tell which house is ours. He has chicken coops all over the side of the hill behind the house."

Well, Ben wasn't interested in the fighting kind of chickens; he had his eye on this young blond chick.

"Where do you go to school?" Ben asked.

"Canton High," she said.

"I go there also. Funny we never met before."

"I'm a junior," she said.

"Well, that is why we haven't noticed each other. I'm a senior; I'll finish school this year."

After more questions between them Ben and Ruth left the store. Ben down the road toward Canton and Ruth and her twin sister up the road to the house with all the roosters.

On Ben's next day at school he was on the "look-out" for his new found friend and possibly his future wife. At a break for changing classes he saw her at her locker; she was getting her books for the next class. She saw Ben and gave him that big smile that girls use to get what they want.

"Hi," she said. "How you doing today?"

"Fine," said Ben. "Ruth... what are you doing this Saturday?"

"Nothing important. Why?"

"Well I was thinking that we could go to the movies at the Strand on Saturday. What do you say?"

"Fine, I love those westerns that they show on Saturday."

This was the start of many future westerns at the Strand Theater.

As the school year continued so did the dating of the new lovers, Ben and Ruth. They were seeing each other between classes and always on the weekend.

Soon the seniors were finished with their high school education and ready for a new adventure in their life. Some chose to go to college take a full time job in the paper mill or venture out into the big world and look around. Ben had other plans.

"Why we don't get married," he said to Ruth.

"But you don't have a job and I need to finish my schooling."

"I have a plan that will take care of both these problems. We will get married, I'll join the Air force and when I come back you will be out of school and we can go out on our own.

"I'll let you know tomorrow," Ruth said.

"OK, I'll see you early tomorrow morning."

Ben or Ruth didn't sleep very much that night. Ben was up early, borrowed his dad's truck and headed to the Stamey Cove and the Trull house. Ruth was expecting him and met him on the front porch. I talked over our plans with mom and dad last night. They didn't think this was a good idea but after a while they said OK. I guess you young people have to leave the nest sooner or later. You may as well do what you your plans are. Ben can go ahead and join the air force; you can stay here at home with us and finish your schooling. When he comes back you and he can start out on your own. Ben smiled from ear to ear. He had himself a future wife.

They decided to have the wedding in South Carolina where there was no waiting period. Buy the license; get married by the JP all in the same building.

"But how are we going to get to South Carolina?" Ruth said.

"I'll find a way," said Ben. "I'll be here early tomorrow morning. Have what things you want to take along."

Away he went in his dad's old pick-up.

His brother-in-law was at his house when he arrived from Stamey Cove with the good news.

"Dad," he said, "do you think your old truck would make it to South Carolina and back?"

"I don't think so and I need it to get to the paper mill and back. You will have to find some other way to get there."

I was listening and I remembered how tough it was for me and his older sister to go anywhere. I had married into his family.

"Ben," I said, "I bought a new Chevy sedan a couple of months ago. You can use it for your wedding trip. I'll drive my old truck until you get back.

"You must be kidding," Ben said. "You loaning me your brand new car?"

"Sure, you can keep it here tonight and get an early start. The tank is full of gas so you won't have to stop on your way. Have fun and be careful with my car."

This was May 27, 1952, in Greenville, South Carolina when Ruth became Ben's "Wife for Life".

The wedding was over and so was the honeymoon. Ben enlisted in the air force and was sent to Japan. Ruth went home to live with mom and dad until Ben returned. There was many letters between Ben and Ruth for the next eighteen months between Canton and Japan. Time went by pretty fast and Ben returned to Canton, North Carolina and his wife, Ruth.

The furlough was over. The packing began for the trip to their new home for the next two years. This was Carswell AFB at Fort Worth Texas. For the next twenty-plus years, Ben and Ruth lived at many bases across the USA. These being at Air Force Bases located at Greenville, South Carolina for seven years. Savannah Georgia, four years, The Philippines, one year, (Ben only). Tacoma, Washington for one year. Rantoul, Illinois for four years. Thailand, one year (Ben Only). Andrews AFB Maryland, three years.

Ben also spent time in Germany, The Azories, and Puerto Rico.

With all this moving they managed to raise a family. The first being a boy, Steve. Another son, Larry and a daughter, Kelly.

Ben retired in 1975; he and Ruth bought a house in Canton and settled in with their children. It took sometime to get used to being a civilian again but they managed.

The children are married and moved away but are close enough that they can visit often.

Ben and Ruth are content with the golden years slipping upon them and are enjoying themselves.

There were many trying times and a lot of hardships to overcome but they made the best of the challenges. It's not this way with newly weds today. Many end in divorce. When they repeat their wedding vows, "Until death we part) they soon forget what they said.

Marriages used to be like this one between Ben and Ruth, and a man had *"A Wife for Life."*

NOTE;

This story is about the life of my brother in law, Benny and his wife, Ruth. All events and places are true as I remember them.

# Odd Names And Places

Have you ever given any thought about odd names that some locations have? Why they are called by this name and what was the reason for their name?

I will name a few that I remember from my childhood days and give the reason for their name as they were told to me.

## *Black Bottom*

There was "Black Bottom" located in a section of Gastonia North Carolina. The ones in Gastonia that worked in one of the many cotton mills lived in a house belonging to

That company. This was considered as part of their benefits by working for them. They were poor working people but there were others that were even in a poorer class. They lived in "Black Bottom".

I was fourteen or fifteen years old when I "Hitch-Hiked" rides to Gastonia from Canton, North Carolina. I went to visit my grandmother. There weren't many cars on the roads in the 30s and I had to do a lot of walking between rides. I did make the hundred mile trip in one day.

My grandma had friends that lived in this area called "Black Bottom". She went to visit once while I was there and I went along. The houses were built very poorly with very few windows and doors. They were small and belonged to owners that rented them to these poor folks for what ever they could pay. I asked why this section at the edge of the town was called "Black Bottom".

I was told that the people that lived here was considered at the bottom of the social ladder and there were several black families living in this area so the name of this section of west Gastonia was "Black Bottom".

There was a song about this place. It went something like this;

When you go down in Black Bottom
Put your money in your shoe
Cause the women in Black Bottom
Make a fool out of you.

There were more to this song, and, as I remember, it became very popular.

## *Greasy Corner*

"Greasy Corner" was also a section of Gastonia. It too was located on the corner of west Franklin Avenue and Vance Street was a bustling business district, serving the residents surrounding the Loray cotton mill. There were restaurants, a theater, and meat market grocery store, garage with gas service, boarding houses and single family homes. The cotton mill was the largest in the south. Years later it was purchased by Firestone the auto tire maker. The name was changed to Firestone. All of "Greasy Corner", except the mill was on Franklin Avenue. The street car tracks were on Franklin. This was the main source of travel from west to east in Gastonia.

I heard several stories as to how it got its name, "Greasy Corner". One was that it came from a restaurant that served greasy food in the early 20th century. Others say it was automotive shops, a lard truck, a slaughter house or slop jars dumped from second-story apartments. There are many theories but most say it was the lard truck.

We will now move to the mountain section of Western North Carolina—Canton.

## Peach Bloom

Peach Tree was an area close to where my family lived near Canton, North Carolina. It was located in a hollow above a bend in the pigeon river near the city limits of Canton, The people living there were working class and lived in homes that were comfortable but only had the bare necessities needed.

The name "Peach Bloom" came about in a very simple way. At some time in the twenty century the owner of this section had a peach orchard along the river and up the hollow. He began to sell off some of the land to people for a home site. Soon all of the peach trees were gone but the name "Peach Tree "remained and it is called this today.

## Home Brew Knob

Now here is a name that will make you thirst. A group of three houses built on the top of a hill that separated the Thickety community and the North Canton / Austin Chapel section. The name given to this place pretty well tells the story of how it got its name. But there was more going on here than the making of beer that was called "Home Brew". There was usually completion between at least two and sometimes all three of the houses for the business of Local lovers of "Moon Shine".

The bootleggers didn't make the "White Lighting" that they sold. Someone would usually bring it from somewhere in the mountains of North Carolina or Tennessee. These haulers were professionals. They would sometimes have two or three cars all looking alike. Only one would have the Moon Shine and when the law men chased them they would split up. All cars going in a different direction. The lawmen didn't know which car to try and catch. They also used smoke screens and nail droppers to stop "The Law" that was chasing them.

## *Frog Level, 1920s*

Our next stop is at a place in Waynesville. At one time when the train station was located at this location nearly all of the business places were located here .Up town as we see it today, did not exist. Only the courthouse and a few houses. Business was booming at "Frog Level".

Where did this name come from? And why the name, "Frog Level"?

This area of Waynesville was located along side of Richland Creek down the hill from Main Street. This is where the railroad tracks were laid and the station built here, until this time the area was a swamp land with very few buildings scattered around but no major development.

This change very quickly after trains began to arrive.

There was a boom in building. In the 1930s and through the 1940s the businesses included, Hardware stores, arm supplies, coal sales, auto dealers and garages, furniture stores, wholesale groceries, warehouses and lumber companies. All these businesses dependent on the railroad.

The area along the creek was always flooding and the local people had said that this place was only fit for frog. So the name "Frog Level" is still the official name of this part of Waynesville, North Carolina.

## Hainty Holler

The next odd name and location will never be easy for me to forget. Why? When I was about ten years old we lived not only above a grave yard but we also lived in one of the houses below it. This was what everyone referred to as, Hainty Holler.

Regardless of which place we lived when going to the Beaverdam School or any other place you would have to go through are around the edge of the grave yard. We had heard so many tales about the haunts that lived on this hill where the dead was buried that we were afraid in the daylight. And at night if there was no other way to get home but to take the trail going through the tombstones.

If I did go this rout you could bet your last nickel that I would run as fast as I could and sometimes with my eyes shut. Let's face it; I was scared to death of ghosts that was in that grave yard. Even today at the age of 86 I avoid a grave yard after dark, Call me a coward if you like. The same ghost that I saw 76 years ago could still be out there.

It is easy to see why this place was called, *"Hainty Holler"*.

## Buzzard's Roost

I will mention one other place that was located up a hollow in a section of Haywood County on Newfound Mountain. This area was called "Buzzard Roost."

No one seems to know who gave this mountain the name or why. Someone said that before all the houses were built on the mountain that for some reason all the buzzards in Haywood and Buncombe county came here to roost after circling all day looking for food. Although the buzzards have left and no longer roost in the trees on the mountain the name has never changed.

I visited the area one time when growing up to be a part of a horse shoe pitching game. There was a family by the name of Cordell that were expert at horse shoe pitching.

I was going to school with one of the younger boys and he invited me to the games.

I looked around for some buzzards but never saw any. I asked where were all the buzzards that everyone said I would see here.

Oh, someone said, I've lived here formerly twenty years and I've only seen a couple of them and they were only passing over. Just because we don't have all the birds that used to be here is not any reason to change our name for this neck of the woods.

The name "Buzzard Roost" suits us just fine.

# Election Time, 1930s

Politics and elections have not changed very much since I was a small boy. The office seeker, the workers and the back room methods are the same. Also the political party has a lot to do with who will be elected for a certain office.

My dad was always very active as a worker in all the elections if it be state or county. We could always tell when there was going to be an election. The candidates would come to our house to talk with dad about working for them before and on Election Day. He listened to all that came by.

He told them he would decide soon. That decision depended on how much money they wanted to spend, how they wanted to spend it and where to spend it. The plan was usually the same every election by all that were running for an office. The more important the job was would mean the one running for it was willing to spend more.

They would begin to tell dad, we will spend this much for haulers. This was paying someone who owned a car a certain amount for every family that he hauled to the voting polls from up the coves of the mountains and anyone that lived to far to walk to the voting place. Very few people owned a car in the 1930s. The rest of the money, you can spend on Election Day at the polls. You spend it anyway you want to, but be sure they vote for me.

The plans were simple. Get out there and buy all the votes you can. We don't want to loose this election. You won't, Dad said. The plans were made and dad had his share of the money that the office seeker could afford.

Election Day, Dad up early, eat a quick breakfast, checked in the trunk of his "A Model" to see if he had enough half pints of "Moonshine" that the Sheriff and the "Bootleggers" had supplied. He would check the list of haulers he had hired and give them their list of where to go for some votes. Off he goes to the poling building near Homer Cagle's grocery store Located where the Beaverdam creek runs into the pigeon river. He hollered back to me, "you can come down about dinner time and I'll buy you a hot dog and a dope." (NE-HI or RC COLA).

"I'll be there," I hollered.

When I arrived at the poling place the crowed was pretty large. This was a day of visiting as well as voting. Some of the people hadn't seen each other since the last election.

One of the haulers pulled into the parking area near the polling building. There were five other people in the car besides the driver. I moseyed over and asked the driver. Where did you get these people? I've never seen them before. He spit out his cud of tobacco and told me this story.

"You know that holler at the head of Beaverdam about half way up the mountain? I was looking for the Bells when I took the wrong road and before I knew it I was in the yard of these peoples' house. 'Can't waste gas,' I said to myself. By this time the man and woman was on the porch."

"Howdy neighbor", I said. "You people planning on voting today? Didn't know there was voting going on, and besides we didn't pay our poll tax this year. Don't matter about the poll tax. If you want vote the feller I am working for will pay the dollar for your tax. Do you have any others living here that are old enough to vote? I guess my three oldest boys could vote but they never have and probably don't know how. Don't make a difference, they will show them how it's done. Now you and the misses get ready and get the boys together. I'll take you there and back and if you want, after you vote I'll take you to town to the café across from the train depot and buy you all a hot dog and a Ne-Hi drink. That is if you vote the right way, they shore make good hotdogs there. Don't put any beans in their chili. Yes sir, they are mighty good."

They were in the car before you could bat an eye.

I went over to where dad was talking to a fellow, I overheard him say, "You take this ballot, put it in your pocket, go inside and get your ballot and go behind the voting curtain. Put the ballot that the clerk gave you in your pocket, go to the ballot box and drop the ballot that I gave you in the box. Come back, give me the blank ballot they gave you and I will give you a 'Bat Wing' of good corn licker or a dollar bill which ever you want."

Off he went to vote.

"How does what you are doing work?" I asked.

Well, before the voting got started I got a blank ballot with all the names on it. I marked the ones I wanted to win. I give the marked ballot to the ones that my haulers bring in, They go inside, get a new ballot, drop the one I marked up in the box, bring me the new ballot and I mark it and give it to the next one.

This system will elect anyone you want to win.

After hearing this I remembered the talk that went around a few years back about a fellow from across the mountain up beaverdam way that was elected as a constable as a joke by these same "Election workers". His name was Billy Stone.

He could neither read or write. Never went to school in his life. After he was elected he did such a good job that none could beat him at the poles. He didn't have a car so he walked everywhere regardless of the distance. He carried a mean looking "Owl Head" pistol and I guess he knew how to shoot it although there was no account of him using it.

He would take the warrants, go to the person who he was serving it on and tell them he had come to take them to jail.

Someone asked once, "Mr. Stone, what does the warrant say I am charged with?"

He replied. "I don't know what the reading up top says but at the bottom it says, 'Fetch You In' so come on, mighty long walk back to the jail."

When I left for WW II in 1942, Mr. Stone was still the constable in the Beaverdam Township section of Haywood County, North Carolina.

The methods of getting votes for who you support have changed over the years but the workers do have a way to influence the voter.

My brother, TJ, has worked at the same voting place as our dad did but not as a "Vote-Getter" but as a judge. Keeping an eye on how things go at the poll to make sure it is run in an honest way. He has done this for over fifty years.

I also have worked on Election Day as the officer of the election since moving to Tennessee. I was also appointed by the state for the position of election commissioner. After one year I was appointed to the position of chairman of the commission.

I guess you could say that politics and elections run in the Family or the old saying, "Like Father-Like Son'. Every American should take an interest in the electing of the ones that are to make decisions that affect the quality and happiness of our lives. Everyone that is eligible should go to the polls on Election Day and vote for the person that they think is best qualified for the job that they seek. They shouldn't let their vote be bought like they were in the "Elections-1930s."

# 'Possum Dinner

The house where we lived in the Thickety section was designed for safety in case the house ever caught fire, It had three bed rooms, a kitchen and what was called a polar or setting room All the rooms had a door between them . The house was built in an "L-shape" with a door that opened to the outside where there was a porch the length of the house.

This house was where a prosperous farmer had raised his family. His name was Chad Wallace. Everyone called him Uncle Chad.

His children were all married and had their own house located somewhere on the Wallis farm. Uncle Chad's wife had died several years ago and he was living with his son. Uncle Chad rented his old homestead along with the barn, apple orchard, chicken house and wood shed. By renting he received a little money and also the house was maintained to keep it from decaying and falling down. We loved to live her better than any other location we had been in the past. The neighbors were real neighbors. Friendly and helpful to each other.

Uncle Chad was a very active person for someone in their seventies. He was lonely living with his son who like a lot of children, were to busy with doing "Their Thing "and had no time for Uncle Chad, an old man.

His new renters did have time for uncle Chad and welcomed his visits. He usually came to our house every day and it would be before dinner time. And of course he was invited to eat with us which he never refused. He had found a home away from home. He became a part of our family during the day time. He had to walk about a mile from his son's house to our house. He took the "Short Cut". Up the high hill, (To small to be called a mountain), down the other side, across the creek and he was ready for a rest in the rocking chair on the porch.

He would always stay around instill dad came home from working in the paper mill.

Uncle Chad had several weaknesses. Two of the greater, (his favorites) was a little drink of moonshine ever so often

And always wanting a good "Possum Dinner". I can find the moonshine but since his wife had died he couldn't get anyone to cook the possum.

Dad solved the moonshine problem by placing a jar in the woods where uncle Chad passed when coming to our house.

He would stop on his way home in the evening and take his median, so he said. His son didn't like for uncle Chad to drink.

He asked where are you getting this whiskey, he asked. You will never know, he said with a smile.

Uncle Chad knew that dad, TJ, my brother and I did a lot of possum hunting. He had seen all the hides (skins) we had on the side of the wood shed. We were curing them for shipment to the fur buyer. One of his visits mom dad and all us children were good possum diner before I pass on. Getting older every day, can't be many more years.

Everyone was quiet. Mom finally spoke up. I ain't cooking any possum but I will make the sweet taters and biscuits, You men can do the cooking of the possum. I'll go to my moms for the day but when I come back there had better not be a mess in my kitchen. And all the dishes and pans better be clean.

Everything for the possum dinner was set except the main course. "The Possum". I and the boys will go hunting one night this week. Just any old possum won't do. Got to get a big old white one. They are always fat.

Come Friday we eat supper, did all of the milking and feeding of the animals. Got a "toe-sack", our lantern and the dog and were off to get that fat possum for Uncle Chad's special dinner before he decided to pass on, as he would say.

We were at the foot of Little Sam Mountain in about thirty minutes. All at once we heard old Buster, our dog, give a few barks.

"Won't be long now," Dad said. "Old Buster has already picked up a trail. Listen at him. Won't be long."

Sure enough old Buster settled down with his tree bark.

"Keep him up there," Dad yelled. "Come on, better hurry. We were up. There he is, don't look too big. Here TJ, hold the lantern and I'll shake him out."

After a couple of shakes the possum was on the ground. I grabbed old Buster to keep him from chewing the possum and running his hide.

"Sure is a small one," Dad said. "Better keep him in case we don't catch any more."

I turned old Buster loose and away he went. It didn't take him long to find another one.

"Better hurry," Dad said. "Not many out this early so we better get him and get back home. I got to work tomorrow and need to get to bed early."

This one was in a bigger tree and up pretty high.

"Here, hold the lantern," he said as he handed it to TJ.

I held the dog and dad began climbing the tree. He was about half way up the tree and he began shaking the top limbs where the possum was setting. All at once he let go of his hold on the limb and down he came.

"WOW," I hollowed. "Sure is a big one, and as white as my hair. Hurry down and put him in the sack before he goes back up that tree."

Dad was down from the tree; the possum was in the sack old Buster was tied so he wouldn't take off and tree another one. We had been gone a little over two hours. We headed back to our house.

After we arrived home there were still things to be done. We had to fix a chicken coop to keep the possums in. We would skin the small one the next day and begin feeding the big one all the buttermilk he could eat. Dad wanted him as fat as we could get him.

Uncle Chad came every day to look at what would soon be his big moment. "The Possum Dinner". Dad told him that he would cook that possum on the next Saturday. He was off from work from Friday until Monday morning.

Mom cooked the sweet potatoes on Friday. Made the biscuits the next morning before leaving for Grand Pa Presley's house. Dad had the possum skinned and dressed when uncle Chad arrived. This was the earliest he had ever come to our house. He was as excited as TJ and I was.

We were looking forward to eating our first possum. According to Dad and uncle Chad they had eat possum many of times.

"One of the best meats," said Uncle Chad.

Mom's big canning pot filled with water was on the wood stove and was soon boiling. In went the meat. He was in one piece. We'll pare boil him for about an hour. When he is tender we will put salt and all the other good stuff on him, laid him in this big baking pan and into the oven for a while. Want him done to the bone.

Uncle Chad wouldn't leave the kitchen although it was really warm from the fire in the cook stove even with the windows and door open. He was going to miss anything. Let's set on the porch while it's cooking, Dad said. I think I'll stay here in the kitchen. Man does that smell good.

About an hour later dad went to the stove, opened the oven, and punched a fork in the side of the then brown possum. Ready to take out, he said. Better set the table, are you boys going to eat with us, he asked? Sure are, I said. Never eat any possum before.

Soon the possum, sweet potatoes and biscuits were on the table. One of you boys go get a jar of buttermilk from the well house. Need something to wash this down.

Uncle Chad and dad wasted no time filling their plate with food. Especially with meat. They began eating like they were starved. I think the two of them slipped around and had a good drink of moonshine. Sort of an appetizer. TJ and I took a little piece of the possum, sweet potatoes and a biscuit. TJ was eating his as though he liked it. I kept chewing the piece I had in my mouth. I couldn't swallow it. It seemed to get bigger and bigger in my mouth. I left the table, went out on the porch where old Buster was laying, took that big bite of possum out of my mouth and gave it to Buster. He wasted no time in swallowing it, looked at me, wagging his tail begging for more.

Uncle Chad, Dad and TJ had finished eating and were cleaning up the table.

"You boys can help wash these dishes. Got to get this place cleaned before your mom comes home."

Everyone except Uncle Chad was washing and cleaning as fast as we could. Soon we were through. Just in time because here comes mom and the two girls, Louise and Leveta. My younger sisters. They had taken sides with Mom about the cooking of possum in her kitchen.

When they walked in the kitchen they began gathering pots and pans. They found a scrubbing brush, some lye soap and headed toward the creek that run through the pasture behind the barn, Going to scrub these pans with sand. Don't want any of that possum grease in my cooking. Out the door and toward the creek they went. It was getting late in the evening and everything was sort of back to normal. Uncle Chad had left for home, the pots and pans put in their right places in the kitchen.

We were all on the porch when dad spoke. "You and the girls sure missed a good dinner. Everything was really good, even if I did cook it."

No one answered him. He smiled a little, took out his pipe, put new tobacco in it and struck a match to light the tobacco.

This was many years ago. I don't recall when Uncle Chad died, but he did get his last wish before parting this earth.

His little drink every now and then, and the most important thing, the *"Possum Dinner."*

# Skunk Doctor

If you live on a farm and have dogs, cats, cows, and other animals, it is almost a must that you know a little about how to doctor them. I had to learn the hard way—by trial and error.

I returned to Western North Carolina after WW II in 1946. First off, I married one of the girls that I had known from my school days at Beaverdam Elementary School. She was one of the five girls from the Young family in Buckeye cove. Marie was the third of eight children in the family. Two years after our marriage our first son, Gary, was born.

Soon it was time to get a larger house. I purchased land, hired carpenters, and before long we were in our new house. Next there was the barn and the purchase of some cattle. We were getting settled in as part-time farmers.

I was working in the paper mill, wiring houses, and keeping a few cattle. Gary was growing up, and when I was home he was tagging after me everywhere I went. I mentioned one day that our young heifer needed de-horning. You wouldn't think a three year old would give this comment any thought, but every evening when I came home from work Gary would ask, "When are we going to cut the horns off that heifer?"

"When I get a pair of clippers and some de-horning tar," I would tell him.

One day I came home from the paper mill and said to him, "As soon as we eat supper, we will cut them horns off that heifer."

His eyes lit up like Christmas tree lights.

Before we were done with our meal he said, "Better hurry Daddy. Soon it'll be dark, and we won't get them horns off."

We left the table and headed to the barn. I chased the young cow into the barn hallway, put a rope halter on her, and tied it as close as I could to one of the locust poles in the hallway.

"Everything is ready," I said. "Better stand back a ways. There may be a little blood."

Gary moved a little, but he was determined to be a part of this job. I placed the clippers on one horn where I wanted to do the cutting. A quick close of the handles, and the first horn was off. Blood was streaming all the way across the hall. When Gary saw this, he began to cry, and he ran out of the barn as fast as he could go, heading to the house and his mother.

The bleeding stopped as soon as I applied the de-horning tar. I finished removing the other horn, put the cow in a stall, gave her some feed, and went to the house. My young helper was as quiet as a mouse.

"You left me," I said.

He didn't answer. There was no more talk about de-horning cattle from him. Gary is past sixty now, and the sight of blood still bothers him.

Our next operation was removing the scent glands from a skunk (or "pole cat" as we called them). The patient was a baby skunk that had just left its mother and was on its own in this big world.

I was at the barn feeding my cows when I heard my little dog barking at something out back of the barn. I took a look, and here was this little skunk acting like she was spraying the stink that a skunk uses for defense. I noticed that there was no smell. I ran after her and grabbed her back legs. I put her in an old rabbit cage that was back of the barn. I would decide later what to do with my little pole cat.

I contacted an animal doctor (a veterinarian) and asked what he charged to de-odorize a skunk.

"Fifteen dollars," he said.

This was out of the question because that was a lot of money in the late forties.

Later I was telling my co-workers at the paper mill about my pet skunk. Someone spoke up and said, "Old Willey in the rigger gang knows how to fix a skunk. He may do it for you."

Off I went to find Willie. "How much to fix my skunk," I asked?

"About five dollars," he said.

"How much for telling me how to do it?" I asked.

"Five dollars," he said.

I went back to work. "I'll operate on that skunk until I find where the scent comes from," I muttered to myself.

I went to the First Aid and Medical Building of the plant. A full-time doctor and two nurses were on duty there. This was where the employees went when they were hurt or sick. I knew one of the nurses real well. She lived in our section called Thickety.

I approached her and said, "Nurse Hipps, I need one of them little sharp knives that you use and a can of ether."

"What in the world are you going to do with a knife and ether?"

"I caught me a little skunk, and I aim to operate on it. When I remove the stink bags, I will have me a pet skunk."

She began to laugh, and went into the next room. She came back and handed me a can of ether and a small knife. "You can keep that knife. It's old and nearly worn out."

I thanked her and left. She was still laughing when I went out of the First Aid office. As I headed for home that evening I was making plans as to how I would go about this operation.

After doing my chores and eating supper I began to get everything together that I might need to fix my skunk. I got a large paper shopping bag, the knife, the ether, and a burlap bag. With Gary at my heels, I headed to the pasture behind the house. I spread the sack on the ground and laid the other things on it. I was ready for "Operation Skunk".

Next I had to go to the cage and get the patient. This I did and we were ready to begin. I opened the paper bag, put the skunk in it, and then poured all of the ether into the bag with her. That pole cat was doing forty around the inside of that paper bag. The ether had wet the bag, a hole came in the side, and the ether was escaping. I was breathing it and was about to go to sleep. Gary had already left me.

I opened the bag and picked up the poor skunk that was not as sleepy as I was. I took her back to the rabbit cage. This day was lost, a failure.

For the next few days I was giving this project some serious thought. I was thinking, "When a dog runs upon a skunk when we are possum hunting, what does the skunk do when spraying his scent? He turns his tail toward his enemy, and his spray comes from the back end. This is where I will look the next time."

My second try at surgery on a skunk was a few days later. The preparation was the same as before, but without the ether. I had brought along a bottle of peroxide instead. I wrapped Whitey, (the name we gave her), in the sack with her rear end sticking out. This was where I would be working.

I had my patient tight between my knees. I poured some peroxide on one of the hips, cut the hair away and made a cut as close to her tail as I could. I looked real close but didn't see anything that would indicate where the stink could come from. I moved to the other side and did the same. Nothing there either.

"Go to the house and have your mother send me a needle and thread," I said to Gary. "And tell her to thread the needle for me."

Off he went as fast as his little legs would move. He returned and handed me the needle with black thread. Mother said that white thread wouldn't look good on a black color. I didn't say anything although I did have objections to the black thread.

I began to sew the places where I had cut. I soon had both sides together and was taking my skunk back to its cage. Another failure at fixing my skunk. But I wasn't through. I would try one more time as soon as the cuts were healed. This would take a few days.

Nearly two weeks had passed since the second operation and I was anxious to give it another try. If I didn't get the stink bags out pretty soon, she would be old enough to start spraying me. This would make the job a lot harder.

I gathered all of my operating supplies together and called to Gary. "Let's go. Time for another operation on Whitey."

Out to the field in back of the house we went. I went to the cage and brought the skunk to where we had worked two times before. I wrapped her in the sack, put her between my knees, and began to look at her back end. This was my lucky day. As I was poking around, out came two small nipples up near the tail. This was it. While they were out like they were trying to spray, I caught one of them between my fingers. I held it out and began to cut around it. Soon I was able to pull a gland out of the top part of the skunk's butt region. When it came completely out I saw that there was a small pouch on the end. I finished this side, and with a little probing I was able to get the one on the other side between my fingers. I soon had both of the "stink sacks" out. The operation was a success.

"We've got us a pet skunk," I said to Gary.

I took Whitey to the basement under the house this time instead of to the cage at the barn. It was safe to have her at the house now that there couldn't be any smell coming from her. I fixed her a bed in a cardboard box in one of the corners of the basement. I also got a pan of water and some baloney from the refrigerator. That cat really loved baloney. I cut it in small pieces, put it in a pan, and set it beside her bed box. She forgot all about the surgery and was only interested in that baloney.

Gary and I left her alone and went upstairs to tell Marie the good news. She didn't seem excited about it at all. She just had a silly grin and a smile on her face.

In about two weeks that skunk was spoiled something awful. She made friends with my little dog. He would bark at her and she would run after him and go through the motions of spraying a scent. I would let her loose in the front yard about every evening so she could locate and dig out grubs and bugs to eat. When it was time to take her back to the basement, I would call her by name and she would come to me.

One evening when she was loose in the yard, I called her and she didn't come to me. I began to look for her but she had disappeared. After a while I gave up looking and went into the house. "Maybe she'll come back," I said to Gary.

"I hope so," he said.

But she never did come back. She was gone for good.

A few weeks later we were watching TV one night when the door bell rang. I went to the door, and there was one of our neighbors.

"Bones", he said. "I saw your skunk run across the road just now."

"Where?" I asked.

"Down by the steps at the road."

I grabbed a flashlight and headed toward where Tom said he saw her. Sure enough, there was a skunk. I didn't look at it very close to see if it was mine. I ran after it, grabbed it by the hind legs and went toward the house. When I was in the yard where Tom was waiting I put the light on it. Was I surprised. This was not my skunk.

"This ain't my cat," I said to Tom. "I'll put it in the cage and decide what to do with it later. Thanks Tom. It could have been Whitey."

I put the skunk in my cage and moved the it from the barn to a spot a long way from the house out in the pasture.

The next Saturday I was off from work at the paper mill. My uncle Doyle came by for a visit. His wife and one of his boys were with him. They came into the house and were showing Marie the new coat that they had bought Jimmy, their son. Jimmy was about the same age as Gary, and they went out to see the skunk.

We were sitting in the living room talking when we heard the boys screaming. The sound was out back of the house. I looked out in the field where the cage with the new skunk was. There in front of the cage were Gary and Jimmy on their knees in front of the cage. They were rubbing their eyes, and the skunk was giving them the full treatment.

"Get away from there," I hollered.

They got to their feet and came running toward the house.

"Don't go in the house!" the women screamed. "Pull all of your clothes off and go to the basement."

The mothers began washing their children, but the smell wouldn't come off. Marie brought clean clothes for the both of them, but they still smelled awful.

My uncle and aunt got Jimmy in their car and headed for home. Marie began giving me a good going over about getting rid of that skunk.

"OK," I said. "I'll get rid of him right away."

I got my shotgun and went to the cage. I carefully opened the door. Out came that skunk, and he headed straight toward me. I ran, thinking he would stop and I could shoot him. But he didn't. He kept coming after me as I went into the basement. Then he came into the basement, too. I ran up the stairs, into the house, out the front door, and around to the basement door. I waited for a few minutes and he finally came out and went into the field behind the house. "Bang!" One shot and he was dead. I would carry him off later.

Everything was soon back to normal around the house, and I was going about my usual duties as were Marie and Gary. My next-door neighbor had a big barn nearby. The foundation of the barn was made from mountain stone stacked but not cemented together. He came over one day and told me he had a family of skunks in his barn. I told him I would take a look as soon as I had time.

I went to his barn the next day and found me a place where I could watch for the skunks. After a little while, here come three little baby skunks out of the rocks. Next out comes the mother. It was my pet skunk, Whitey.

I called her but she wouldn't come to me. She and the little ones scampered back behind the rocks. Now I knew why she went missing. She had run off to find her a husband and start a family.

This was not the end of my being a "skunk doctor." I deodorized several skunks for other people. I never charged anyone for doing this for them. I still have that little knife that Miss Hipps gave me fifty plus years ago, but. I don't do surgery anymore for fear of getting rabies.

# Afterword

The stories that are in this book, are a continuation of the ones in my first book, Out West and Back. My children, grandchildren, and others who read my first book asked that I continue telling stories that were told to me as a child by my older relatives and friends.

As I wrote these stories, I made them as accurate as I could. But, at the age of eighty-six, all the details of the past are sometimes hard for me to recall.

I am a native of North Carolina, and I grew up and spent my earlier years in the mountains of Western North Carolina. All of the stories and ballads of the people from these mountains were based on something that actually happened in their lives. They were storytellers, and they passed on their experiences to the younger generation while everyone was gathered around the dinner table or in front of the fireplace at night. They were storytellers, and I was one of their students. After all the years that have passed, I have never forgotten that I am a storyteller.

# Biographical Note

Charles C Fletcher, the author of *The Panther on Cold Mountain*, was born April 1, 1922 in North Carolina. He was educated in public schools. He continued his schooling after returning to North Carolina after WW II and earned a degree in industrial electrical engineering. This book is a continuation of the stories that are in his first book. This is his way of answering the many questions from his grandchildren. All events and places are as accurate as remembered by an Eighty six year old. He hopes the readers of this book enjoy the stories as well as he did writing them.